*Mignon~~~~~~~~~~~~~~~~~~~~~~earning
about cro~~~~~~~~~~~~~~~~~plans.*

Robert laugh~~~~~~~~~~~~~~~~~, ne said. "It
takes firmnes~~~~~~~~~~~ a true eye. Let me show you
how to hold the mallet."

He bent Mignonne's shoulders and showed her how to
position her feet apart for the proper stance. Standing
behind her, he closed his arms around her. His fingers
shaped her wrists and placed her hands on the mallet.

She could feel the texture of his crisp linen coat through
her soft crepe. Her ruffled sleeves fell back, baring wrists
and fingers that tingled with his touch. His tanned face
was close enough to inhale the warm fragrance of her
porcelain skin. His breath felt sweet on the nape of her
neck.

Softly, he brushed his mustache across her spine.
Stiffening, they stood still, holding the mallet. Then, ever
so gently he kissed the curve at the back of her neck.

Feelings she had never experienced were bubbling up
like the geyser spring. Turning in his arms, she looked
into his face. He was as shaken as she.

People were chattering and milling about all around
them. It seemed stranged, special, that although they had
contrived moments in the moonlight, they had waltzed in
each other's arms, they had felt only a sense of waiting.
Now, amid a crowd, in broad open daylight, in a moment
unplanned, unexpected, binding currents passed between
them.

There was no more holding back. Whether it brought
joy or pain, Mignonne knew in that moment that she was
deeply in love with Robert Edgefield.

JACQUELYN COOK is a veteran inspirational romance author whose extensive research brings alive the gracious living of the people of Macon, Georgia, during the late 1800s.

Books By Jacquelyn Cook

HEARTSONG PRESENTS

HP17—River of Fire
HP27—Beyond the Searching River

Don't miss out on any of our super romances. Write to us at the following address for information on our newest releases and club information.

Heartsong Presents Reader's Service
P.O. Box 719
Uhrichsville, OH 44683

Rivers Rushing
to the Sea

Jacquelyn Cook

A sequel to *Beyond the Searching River*

Heartsong Presents

For Samantha, Matthew, Jessica,
and Michael

PZ3. C6

ISBN 1-55748-502-X

RIVERS RUSHING TO THE SEA

one

Mignonne Wingate's brown eyes misted as trumpet-like notes from the pump organ announced the wedding march. Music suspended over the garden of Great Hill Place. Powder-puff asters, sparkling as blue as the October sky, and pink chrysanthemums, wafting elusive fragrance, lined the path to the wedding bower in the heart of the garden. To the ringing notes of Mendelssohn, Libba Ramsey, the bride, approached the altar, weeping for joy.

A nameless restlessness stirred Mignonne. She glanced at her parents. Holding hands, Lily and Harrison Wingate radiated contentment, peace. Blinking back her tears, Mignonne yearned for such a love.

Through wet lashes, she glimpsed Paul. Tall, with dark auburn hair, he was the handsomest man she had ever seen. *Now that he has lost Libba to Daniel,* she thought, *maybe he will notice me.*

Paul Morley treated her like a child, as did everyone in her protected world. But this past June of 1877, she had turned seventeen. Her raven-haired beauty made her look mature. She was ready to taste life for herself.

The small organ wheezed. Sarah Lois Wadley worked the foot pedals patiently. They caught.

Music swelled, then settled over the guests seated in the paved nook around the garden sculpture of the Greek messenger Hermes.

In this enchanted setting, Mignonne felt herself wrapped in a "Midsummer Night's Dream."

The ceremony ended with prayer. Everyone was kissing the bride.

Hands still clasped beneath her little, pointed chin, head still bowed, Mignonne looked up through the fringe of bangs brushing her thick, dark brows. Her sparkling eyes, widened by lashes fanning from the corners, gave her an expression at once innocent, pixie-like, beguiling.

Charmed, Paul came to her. With enough of a bow to make it look like a gentlemanly greeting, he took her white-gloved hand and pressed his mustached mouth in a slow kiss.

"Has anyone ever told you that you look like a little French doll?" he murmured softly so no one else could hear.

The pink of her cheeks deepened prettily. "Papa's people were French." Her voice, soft and sweet, slid over syllables like molasses melting over hot biscuits. "They were Napoleonic exiles who lost their claim to the throne of France and settled in Demopolis, Alabama."

Paul's appreciative look made her glad she had chosen her pink organza. The sheer silk clung to her slender neck and flared in a ruffle that kissed her chin and earlobes. The wide hat, sitting squarely atop her long, black hair, was adorned with organza puffs shaped like roses. As his dark eyes swept down over her dress with its sophisticated slim skirt, bustle, and train, Mignonne's breath caught in her throat. She could not let it go until his sister joined them, breaking the intensity of his gaze.

"H'lo Minnie," Endine Morley said. "May I introduce my friend Zachary Jones? Y'all come join us for refreshments. We should raise a cup of punch to Queen Victoria."

Mignonne blinked at the cryptic remark. Endine had frizzy pink hair, a thousand freckles, and a sarcastic tongue. No one ever knew what to expect from her, but Mignonne, open-hearted, ready to love everyone, counted her a friend.

Climbing the granite steps of the terraced garden, they followed the wedding party up the walkway between landscaped levels lined with pungent, bittersweet boxwood.

Great Hill Place, the favorite home of the Wadley family, was a cotton plantation at Bolingbroke in the rolling red hills near Macon, Georgia. The white house, like its family members, was tall, plain, even austere. With its southern porch extended by a northern stoop, it was unique.

Towering oaks surrounded it. The trees seemed matched in size and power by Colonel Wadley. Hearing his gruff, New Hampshire twang, Mignonne stepped aside to let him pass. She felt slightly afraid of the prominent man who was president of the Central Rail Road and of the Ocean Steamship Company. Unsmiling and stern, he was, but handsome with his straight nose and crown of white hair. And his huge hands were gentle as he helped his wife, Rebecca, into the house. She moved with the groping steps of one who hoped no one realized she was going blind.

The party milled about the shining, polished floors of the central hall. In the living room Mignonne admired a handsome secretary of dark cherry. Atop this was set an enormous Chinese bowl. Everything was simple, dignified, not calculated to impress. Current styles called for overstuffed and overdone. The Wadleys preferred genuineness.

Their eldest daughter, Sarah Lois, moved about welcoming guests. At thirty-three, past the marriageable age, she lived through the lives of others.

She led them to the tremendous dining table, voluptuous with food. Simmering sausages, dainty sandwiches, exotic fruits, and cream-filled pastries were served from piece-after-matched-piece of shining coin silver.

"What lovely silver," said Mignonne as Sarah Lois refilled her punch cup from a pitcher with a design of a grape arbor protecting a flock of pheasants.

The tall, angular woman smiled down at her. Arresting brown eyes, which snapped with intelligence from beneath straight brows, kept her face from being plain. She moved with a rustle of taffeta that gave off the scent of lavender sachet.

When she spoke, her enthusiasm showed how

she doted upon her famous father. "The silver was given to Father as a testimony of esteem. He was especially pleased that the inscription is not only from railroad officers but also from mechanics and employees." She pointed out the train engraved on the silver as she served Mignonne cake.

Mignonne bit into the rich, buttery wedding cake moist with fruits and nuts. It was difficult to eat with Paul's eyes tingling upon her. At least she did not have to speak. Zachary and Endine were debating a new invention he had seen demonstrated when he went to Philadelphia for the Centennial Exhibition.

"Dr. Alexander Graham Bell's telephone is the most amazing—"

Endine interrupted. "I can't imagine what earthly good it is. How could the person you want to talk with know to be at the other end of the line?"

"That is a problem. But they're trying different call bells."

She pursed her lips. "It's just a squeaky little plaything!"

Listening to them, Mignonne wished that she could travel. Of course, southern belles no longer made Grand Tours of Europe. She wouldn't hurt Papa by even asking, but it would be nice to see this country.

She smiled encouragingly at Zachary, who was looking a bit dampened by Endine's sarcasm. "It must be so excitin' to see new things. I long to travel."

"Why, Minnie, you were practically born on a steamboat."

"That's different. When your father is captain and the riverboat is named for you, the passengers and crew all talk about the cute things you did as a two-year-old. You can't grow up! I've never been beyond the Chattahoochee."

Paul, who had been languishing, came suddenly erect. "Endine!" he said in a deep, vigorous voice, "Why can't she go with us?"

Endine's yellow eyes narrowed. "We're fixing to leave on a trip. Cousin William is taking Cud'en Rebecca to New York to a specialist. Paul works for him. But I'm just going, and I need a companion. There's lots of room in the president's private car. If you went it would make things—interesting."

Mignonne wondered at the intent of Endine's tone and the slant of her glance at her brother, but she was too delighted at the prospect of being with Paul to worry about deciphering the strange girl.

"Oh, Mama," Mignonne caught Lily's arm as she passed. "You remember Paul Morley and Ahndeen." She pronounced the unusual name carefully to remind her mother. "And this is Zachary. The Wadleys are taking a trip, and Endine has invited me to go along as her companion. Oh, please, I do so want to go!"

She looked at her mother beseechingly. Lily had grown more beautiful with maturity. Her hair, although not as black as Harrison's and Mignonne's, had darkened instead of graying. She remained vivacious. Always sensitive to the needs of others, she possessed an insight that Mignonne now found unnerving. Lily could see that she was falling in love with Paul.

Just when she should be reassuring her mother of her trustworthiness, she blushed and her full lips pouted. The boys of Eufaula were always buzzing around her, but they seemed like her brother, Beau. Paul, twenty-four, was a man.

Lily was hesitating. "I'm afraid it would be an imposition on the Wadleys."

"Not at all," interposed Sarah Lois, who had paused for a cup of punch now that all were served. "There's plenty of room in Father's car. Mother and Father would be pleased to have Mignonne along to keep Endine out of mischief."

Lily frowned doubtfully. "Still, I'm not sure that—"

"I'll be there to keep an eye on everyone," Sarah Lois assured her.

"Please, Mama. Now that the Civil War is in the past, everything is changing!"

Mignonne immediately regretted her choice of words. Lily was standing with her mouth open, and she feared her mother would start spouting Scripture about how God never changes.

"What's all this?" Harrison Wingate's quiet voice interrupted.

Relieved that her father had appeared, Mignonne turned to him. Tall, distinguished by graying temples, he watched her with a twinkle as her explanation poured out.

Tweaking his mustache in amusement, he looked deeply into Lily's eyes in silent communion. With one of his Gallic gestures, he lifted his hand in the image of tossing a baby bird from the nest and puffing air beneath its wings.

Imperceptibly, Lily nodded.

He turned to Miss Wadley. "Mignonne is right. Her whole life has been lived during the War Between the States and the Reconstruction. Now that President Hayes is removing the Federal Army of Occupation from the South, we can enjoy our lives again. It should be safe for her to travel and see what the world is like."

And so it was settled.

There was a sudden flurry when the bride and groom prepared to leave. They ran through a shower of rice and drove away in a buggy dragging old shoes and bearing a sign, "Just Married."

Assorted Wadley grandchildren and fine hunting dogs, setters, hounds, and one three-legged mutt ran down the lane after them, jumping, leaping, mingling cheers, barks, and joyous shouts.

Mignonne's trunk, which had been well packed for the trip from her Eufaula, Alabama, home to this middle Georgia plantation, was brought from the hotel. Shadows lengthened. Guests departed. Adults collapsed. Children and dogs still ran about in high excitement.

Mignonne removed her hat and gloves, ready to

stay. Her eyes, wide in her delicate face, lifted to Paul expectantly.

With a deep chuckle, he plucked rice from the dark hair spilling over her shoulders. "If you're so interested in new inventions, let me show you my hydraulic machinery that brings running water to the house."

Eagerly she followed him back to the formal garden. The entrance was guarded by tall sentinels of Italian cypress, which Sarah Lois had brought back from her tour of Europe when she was young. Catching the satin loop that lifted the train of her dress with one hand, Mignonne gave him the other. They ran down the smooth steps.

Colors and shapes of flowers on each inviting terrace passed in a blur, but her heightened senses absorbed the odors: the musky boxwood, the clean, spicy scent of the man who was leading her pell-mell.

"Wait, oh, wait!" she gasped, clutching the ruffled cape that had come untied and was threatening to slip from her bare shoulders. "You're going too fast."

Paul laughed. He let her catch her breath in the center of the garden that still looked like a wedding bower. He showed her the prized sculpture of the slender youth whose hat and sandals were adorned with small wings for flight over land and sea.

Their way wound intriguingly downward. When they came to the end of the controlled stone path, their feet moved soundlessly over soft, brown pine straw. Natural woodland enclosed them. The mood of the garden changed. Dainty flowering trees gave place to their towering forest brethren. Leaves rustled as squirrels scampered ahead of them. Wandering at will along the dimly seen path, Paul and Mignonne reached a small creek where laughing water leapt over rocks, kissed yearning ferns, dashed heedlessly on.

Click-*chug*. Click-*chug*. Click-*chug*. In the green stillness, the sharp staccato sounded a startling note.

Frightened, Mignonne stiffened, but Paul's arm came around her, comforting, helping her over a fallen log. She shivered with delight at his touch.

He explained the hydraulic machinery while she watched him adoringly. "The weight of the water tumbling over the small waterfall presses a lever and clicks the valve shut. The recoil hurls the water against an inner valve, opening it."

"You mean the water pumps itself with no other source of energy?" She looked up at him with her face full of wonder.

"The principle was discovered by one of your countrymen named Pascal. I've only adapted it." He grinned proudly. "The water forces into this pipe and up the hill to the cistern. Then gravity gives strong pressure." He squeezed her hand. "Come, let me show you."

With clasped hands swinging between them, they crossed the open meadow to a grand, round column of brick encompassing the water tank. Tall, strong like the members of the family, the tower was architecturally beautiful. Did the high-arched doorway and the slender spiral of stairs she glimpsed inside lead only to a waterworks?

Lifting her skirt demurely, Mignonne stepped on the first tread as he indicated. Suddenly she realized that once she entered the steel spiral, she would be trapped.

She turned, looked down at him. How handsome he was! She wanted to put her fingers in that thick auburn hair, to feel that charming mustache upon her lips in her first real kiss.

Drawing a long, deep breath, she waited. Mama's voice was in her ear reminding how Timothy was cautioned by Paul to flee youthful lusts and call upon the Lord out of a pure heart.

As graciously as possible, she pushed both hands against his chest and laughed merrily.

"You have taken all my breath away. I believe I'll save this climb for another day." She smiled impishly. "I just bet Miss Sarah Lois is looking for me."

Undaunted, Paul brushed his mustache lightly across her lips, but he lifted her down and released her.

Night had fallen. Twinkling stars seemed near. As they walked down the hill and across the open meadow toward the house, Mignonne realized that leaving her childhood behind and traveling north with Paul would be a hazardous journey.

two

The engine, named—W. M. Wadley sped across Georgia at an amazing forty miles an hour. Rattling over zigzagging rails, the train plunged through thick, dark forest that hovered close around the track. Chugging up the red clay hills of the rolling Piedmont, the train catapulted down as if the cars were pushing the engine. Whistling, bell tolling, it conquered the last hill and shot onto the flat coastal plain.

"Oooh!" Mignonne exclaimed, blinking at the sunlight dancing on open fields so white with cotton they looked as if they were covered with snow. "It's as if we're in a different world!"

Paul grinned. "I'm going to show you things you've never even dreamed of." His big, brown hand slipped over her small white fingers resting on a backgammon board set on a small table beside a window.

Seated comfortably in Colonel Wadley's private car, the family members were employed at various pursuits. Wadley worked at a large table buried in documents, but his glance darted out the window to check each grade and crossing. Rebecca knitted contentedly. Sarah Lois wrote in her diary. Endine was stretched out engrossed in one of George

Sand's scandalous novels.

Mignonne had not been an apt pupil as Paul tried to teach her his favorite game. Now her attention left the backgammon entirely and focused on the landscape passing slowly like an unfolding fan.

Workers in colorful layers of clothing pulled burlap bags through rows of shoulder high plants as they picked the fluffy bolls. This was the prized Sea Island cotton. The cotton crop still affected the entire economy of the South.

The whistle blasted a long, warning ummmmm.

"Ohh, look." Mignonne adroitly removed her fingers from Paul's hand and pointed to a liver-spotted hound sitting at the muddy crossroad. Raising his muzzle skyward, he bayed a mournful howl. Another dog, a large black mutt, planted his feet firmly, bristled his hair, and barked at the intruding train.

They laughed together.

"Dogs bark at steamboats, too, you know. Once Foy almost wrecked the *Mignonne Wingate* because he judged the river's course by the sound of a barking dog that was always chained on a certain bluff. One dark night, the dog moved to the water's edge. He had broken his chain."

"That's one reason steamboats are losing the race for business to the railroads. Our course is always laid out straight and sure."

"And you never have to stop and wait for a rain to make the water rise over a sandbar."

"No. Trains master every situation," he boasted.

"Nowadays instead of waiting for the sun to be directly overhead to set their clocks at noon, country folks can set them anytime of day by the trains. We are always on schedule. Sun time was fine when ignorant folks stayed on farms and never went anywhere. Now, time signals are flashed to all stations on the railroad for engineers to set their watches. The whole world is moving fast to keep on the railroad's schedule."

His arrogant gaze roamed over her. "But are we missing the romance?" His voice became low, caressing. "On the floating palace of your riverboat, I could be holding you in my arms, dancing to the throb of violins."

Mignonne cut her eyes at him coquettishly. "But I hear music in the clacking rails. A new, a faster song. Rails rushing to the sea. Oh, yes, this is exciting, too."

Whistling for a station, the engine slowed. Mignonne was glad this was a working trip because Paul got out at every stop to help Colonel Wadley check bridges and roadbed. Her heart was matching the bum-bump, bum-bump of the train over the rails. She needed the moments away from Paul to pull back from his spell.

"This is the town of Wadley," said Sarah Lois, smiling at the daydreaming Mignonne. "Would you like to get out and walk about? One's bones do get tired from the train's constant jerking."

"Yes, ma'am."

Mignonne put on her hat with its youthful, turned-back brim. She had made a mistake in choosing her outfit. The dainty, sprigged muslin, which had been fine on the porch of the riverboat, had become smudged with smut and cinders from the puffing engine. She felt like a naughty child too mussed to attend the party.

Sarah Lois, on the other hand, cut an imposing figure as they walked along the street. In her grey serge traveling costume, she looked upholstered in the odd, goose-shaped silhouette of the day. The straight skirt, covered with an apron front that pulled back into a tasseled bustle, allowed her to walk briskly.

Noticing Mignonne's appreciative appraisal of her stylish attire, the older lady said, "With this new freedom both from cumbersome hoop skirts and from restrictive pre-war mores, ladies need no longer remain indoors with fans and smelling salts. We can take part in the scene."

As she swept along past hotels and boarding houses for the crews who worked in the repair barn or on the railroad, the huge ostrich plumes that trimmed her high-crowned Gainsborough hat fluttered, and the mauve taffeta ribbons streamed out behind. The wide brim of the black velvet hat dipped low over one snapping dark eye and gave her a sardonic expression.

"They used to call the town Shakerag," she said, laughing. "Presumably because a prospective passenger had to wave a rag to stop the train. The

Louisville and Wadley Railroad runs up from here to Louisville. At first they wouldn't allow the railroad. They were afraid the steaming locomotive would frighten the children and chickens."

Endine laughed.

Mignonne murmured, "So many things are named for Colonel Wadley."

"Yes, also a town in Louisiana and a tugboat, but the only thing he ever brags about is that he came down from New Hampshire with his anvil on his back. Starting as a blacksmith, he rose to superintendent of the Central Rail Road and Banking Company.

"Then came the war, and the president of the Confederacy, Jefferson Davis, appointed him colonel and adjutant general to superintend the railroads. Rail transportation was vital to the war. The Confederacy was broken when Yankee General Sherman took Atlanta and marched to the sea destroying the railroad."

"Tomorrow," Endine interrupted, "I'll show you where Libba saw the Yankees prying up the rails and twisting them like bow ties around the pine trees in the Ogeechee Swamp."

Sarah Lois nodded. "The child was very nearly as scarred as the landscape. After the war, Father was asked to rebuild the three hundred miles of destroyed railroad as president of Georgia's Central. Now, in this new era of railroading, his name is equivalent in the South with that in the East of New York Central tycoon Cornelius Vanderbilt."

Night was falling. The train rolled easily through Georgia's sandy low country. Mignonne watched flickering lights filtering through mist. Suddenly it was dark, and the window mirrored her expectant face. The coach hurled through blackness as if it were a separate entity from the world. Lost in thought, she heard the voices behind her as a hum.

The sound changed. Conversation lapsed into aimless murmurs as the hungry family eyed the white-linened table and moved about restlessly.

Prince announced dinner. Mignonne was seated at the opposite end from Paul. Disappointed, she wondered why Sarah Lois, who had seemed friendly this afternoon, had deliberately separated her from Paul.

The white-haired butler, who had been a part of the family since 1863, began serving elegant food.

The fruit course, a fluted orange in a footed, silver orange cup, was set before her. From the array of silver forks and spoons at her plate, she selected a pointed orange spoon. She held it poised, swaying with the rhythm of the train, hoping she would not upset the orange cup. Concentrating, she was unaware of Colonel Wadley's conversation with Paul until one word frightened her.

"I hazard we are in for war."

Mignonne paled. War had been a dim part of her babyhood, but the last twelve years of the Reconstruction were vivid: the fears and tensions of the carpetbaggers' rule, the degradation of Blue Coat soldiers with their rifles and bayonets everywhere.

Her father's family had lost most of their fleet of steamboats in the war. She knew that they were forced to borrow money to rehabilitate ruined plantations, but she had never realized how they used only old things and watched every penny until she witnessed the Wadley's wealth. They had eaten plenty. She liked the peas and corn from Mama's garden. She had never lacked for anything. She had always felt protected, loved. Loved by everyone in Eufaula.

Orange juice dribbled down her wrist. She thought the d'oylies, small fringed napkins, were meant to protect the white dinner napkins from fruit stains, and she wiped her hands carefully before she cleared her throat to speak to Colonel Wadley.

"Sir, do you mean more civil war?"

"No, my child," he replied in his terse twang. "I meant at the stockholders' meeting tomorrow. A northern syndicate is rapidly acquiring controlling interest of the Central's stock. It's a Wall Street group whose obsession is synonymous with this new industrial age that has replaced our nation's agrarian innocence—wealth at any cost. My nemesis, General E.P. Alexander, will be there. He had no interest in the crippled road, but now that I've built it into a model system, he's threatening my power. But I stand ready to fight."

Prince presented a silver waiter of roasted squab. Wadley paused to take the serving spoon and fork and lift the whole bird onto his plate.

Mignonne, her face bright with intelligence and

interest, kept her attention upon him, and he resumed speaking.

"I hazard you wonder why I, a New Englander, espoused the Confederate cause. It was from both feeling and principle. Railroads were a chief cause of the Civil War. The North wanted power in the federal government. They wanted federally sponsored railroads. The South insisted upon rights of states and individuals."

He laughed grimly at his own intensity. "I'm still fighting that war. Speculators are building railroads from nowhere to nowhere. Fortunes have been made, both honestly and dishonestly, through federal government grants to railroads in the West. Men have risen from nothing to fantastic wealth and power. Fortunes for the few, hurt for the many— giving railroading a bad name. I'm striving to preserve the Central for the honest citizens who built it to haul cotton to the wharves at Savannah for the economic good of all."

He rubbed his big hands together as if already preparing for the fight.

When the elaborate meal ended, Paul took Mignonne's elbow and said, "Let's go out and get some air."

Colonel Wadley's car was attached to the end of the freight train. When they stepped out the rear door they were on the observation platform, swinging through the darkness. Alone. The moon was rising.

"Ohh, it looks like a big orange. How beautiful!"

"Not half as beautiful as my petite Mignonne."
He lifted one shining black curl from her shoulder
and rolled it in his fingers. "Tomorrow I'll show
you a city bigger, finer than anything you can imagine. Savannah was a hundred years old before your
little ole Eufaula saw the last of the Indians."

Emotion closed her throat. Unable to speak, she
looked up at him, waiting. He was so tall. So handsome.

"And, I'll show you the Atlantic Ocean. You can't
imagine how big it is. Strong. Often violent. Not at
all like your gentle green Gulf."

Mmmmm! The warning of the whistle drifted
over them as the rushing train rounded a long curve.
The car lurched, but Paul's steadying arm slipped
around her waist.

The clacking music of the rails seemed to be
pounding from within her. She stood on tiptoe,
ready to receive his kiss.

Endine's scornful voice interrupted. "Prince has
made up the berths, and Auntie Sarah Lois is calling bedtime. I'll take the upper berth this time and
give you the lower. You'd probably fall out the top
since you're such a greenhorn."

three

Sunlight, streaming through the tall, arched windows of the handsome new depot that Wadley, himself, had designed, welcomed them to Savannah. Awed, Mignonne looked up at the twenty-three-foot ceilings. She easily believed it when they told her this was the finest and most complete railroad station in the United States.

They walked outside into a world of cotton. Jute-wrapped bales were pile high. Brought from the warehouses at Macon by the freight train that had pulled the president's coach, they were unloaded and stacked on mule-drawn wagons to be taken to the warehouse-lined Savannah River; from there steamships carried them to England and the looms of Liverpool.

Paul smiled indulgently at Mignonne's excitement. "The factors trading at the Cotton Exchange on Savannah's waterfront set cotton prices for the world," he told her. "It's only fitting because it was here at Mulberry Grove Plantation that Eli Whitney invented the cotton gin."

Colonel Wadley proceeded to his office on the waterfront, leaving Paul to escort the ladies to the Wadley's house.

Mignonne looked eagerly from the carriage

window as the horses clop-clopped along the brick paving of the tree-lined boulevard called Liberty Street. The old row houses with plain fronts rising directly from the sidewalks were different from anything she had ever seen.

"The simple exteriors conceal elegant interiors," Rebecca told her.

"But how can they live without gardens?"

"Peep through that wrought iron gate," Sarah Lois said, smiling. "In the rear are exquisite gardens—small and intimate."

The carriage turned left on Bull Street, and Mignonne decided that Savannah, itself, was a garden. The thoroughfare meandered around squares of beautifully landscaped parks. Tall, dark, romantic magnolia trees stood beside low live oaks wearing spreading evergreen gowns and gray lace shawls of Spanish moss on their open arms. Beneath the trees, gentlemen with long flapping coattails strolled with ladies attired in colorful slim skirts with fancifully adorned bustles and tremendous hats trimmed with flowers and plumes. Smiling promenaders stopped their chatting to wave at the Wadleys in the passing carriage.

"The people and the trees seem equally dressed up and gracious," said Mignonne with a twinkle.

"Long ago the squares were filled with English soldiers fighting to protect their settlement from the Spanish in Florida," replied Sarah Lois. "General Oglethorpe landed here in 1733 bringing families armed with agricultural implements, seeds, ideals of religious freedom, and a motto I subscribe to: not for self but for others."

Mignonne looked from the churches welcoming on every corner to her chaperone's plain face. Yes, Sarah Lois, like Savannah, practiced what she taught.

That afternoon while the older ladies napped, the girls explored. The old city enchanted Mignonne. A slow, easy grace showed on the surface, but underneath, an excitement, a current, undulated. Here things were happening.

By the time they returned home, news of the Wadleys' arrival had spread. All manner of social invitations were extended. Everyone knew that Rebecca delighted in people and parties.

The house burst with energy when Wadley entered boasting how masterfully he had handled the stockholders' meeting.

"I stayed in control in spite of opposition from directors. I was determined never to relinquish my convictions of right and wrong. I negotiated a lease which guaranteed a certain dividend to stockholders even in the face of complications arising about western freights." He beamed. "I surprised them by agreeing to remain as manager of the leased road as long as my services would be of value. I hazard my adversaries were astounded."

Rebecca patted him lovingly. "People have wrongly attributed a grasping spirit of domination to you. Now they'll see your sacrifice and overlooking of personal ambition. They'll know, as I do, your true dignity."

Mignonne could not fully comprehend their words, but the scowl contorting Paul's handsome face puzzled her more. Eagerly she followed him into the tiny jewel of a garden, which was walled from prying eyes.

"What's wrong?"

He snorted in disgust. "Other railroad magnates are amassing unbelievable personal fortunes. They'll laugh at Cousin William's placing the welfare of his company before his private interest. New York railroad men make wild profits by manipulating stocks. If I could deal with the Bulls and Bears, I'd have so much money I could do what *I* want to do."

"I don't understand."

"Cousin William won't speculate in stocks. He simply borrows what he needs from the bank and pays back loans. If he knows stocks are going up or down, he keeps the knowledge to himself. But if I could find out what plans are made at board meetings and know what to buy or sell—there's no telling how rich I'd get. Big Jim Fisk, Jay Gould, and Daniel Drew swindled control of the Erie Railroad from Cornelius Vanderbilt by selling stock illegally." He laughed. "Of course, old Commodore Vanderbilt was a master at bribing legislatures and 'watering stock.' It's all part of the game of big business."

"Watering stock?"

Paul grinned shrewdly. "One of Wall Street's master speculators is former cattle drover Daniel Drew. Out West he fed his cattle quantities of salt and waited until they reached the market to give them water. That creates a false appearance of weight. The term followed him to New York where he—"

Mignonne was frowning and shaking her head.

He cupped her chin in his big hand. "Don't worry your pretty little head trying to understand man talk."

Her lips thrust out in a pout, and her eyes glinted angrily. She understood all too well the crookedness he was admiring.

But Paul had forgotten his anger over business. A devilish look came into his dark eyes. "My, my, don't we look grown up for tonight's party."

She had chosen her lavender gown instead of her usual childish pink to impress him with her sophistication. The snug-fitting basque and side panels were of lavender silk. The sleeves and bustle and train were elegant puffs of purple grenadine. The neckline was low, heart-shaped. Her mother had filled it in with a nosegay of silk violets, which Mignonne had been tempted to remove. Now, uncomfortable in the intimacy of Paul's gaze, she was glad she had not.

Outside the garden wall, a creak of springs and the jingling of horses' harnesses indicated carriages were ready to take them to the dinner party.

"Come on, my petite. Tonight you shall have your fill of crab, oysters, shrimp, and all manner of delights from the sea."

But when they arrived at the party in a glittering mansion on the square, Paul treated Mignonne and Endine as if they were his baby sisters. Then he left them entirely.

The next morning, behaving attentively again, Paul told the girls he would take them to the Ocean Steamship Office and show them something special. He had a buggy, which meant they were squeezed close together on the one narrow seat.

As Paul drove the horse down the steep incline to the waterfront, he explained the cobblestones paving the road were ballast brought on early ships from England.

The big brick Cotton Exchange had blocked the view. Suddenly the bustling harbor was spread before Mignonne. The Savannah River, muddy red, wide and deep, made her recall her dear shallow green Chattahoochee leaping laughingly over stones and sandbars. But instead of small, flat-bottomed steamboats, these were huge, masted steamships flying flags of many nations. She leaned forward, forgetting homesickness in the excitement of new things. The river was reaching out toward the Atlantic Ocean. She smiled at the sea gulls wheeling white against the sky.

At the Ocean Steamship Wharves above the city, they found Colonel Wadley out supervising the building of two fine iron steamers, *City of Macon* and *City of Savannah*.

Wadley ushered them into his office as if they were important guests and he had nothing to do but entertain them.

"I want to show you this new invention," he said. "I predict it will be in general use within the present generation."

They waited expectantly while Mr. Richardson attached the telegraphic instrument to a new telephone. He pressed a doorbell-like button to signal the other end of the line.

Colonel Wadley took the wooden case of the combined receiver and transmitter. His gruff voice boomed. "Who is at the other end of the line?"

"Conners here, sir, at the Bay Street office of Richardson and Barnard."

The man was a mile away! Astonishment silenced everyone in the room. Then, someone led a cheer.

At last Mignonne's turn came to speak into the telephone. Unsure, she held up the wooden tube with a round end that made it look like a butter stamp.

The door burst open. A red-faced man shouted, "Come quick, Colonel Wadley, sir. The workmen are starting a riot!"

four

The telephone cord dangled around Mignonne. Riots had been too much a part of her life. Remembering Foy, her mother's handsome young brother who had been shot in a riot wresting their local government from the carpetbaggers and scalawags, she feared for Paul.

She was about to drop the telephone and move to Paul's comforting side when Wadley's penetrating eyes stopped her.

"Tell Conners to send the police!" the big man commanded her. Then he charged out the door.

"I. . ." Mignonne held the strange object away from her. Feeling silly talking into something that looked like a wooden stamp used to imprint designs on butter, she raised the transmitter to her lips. "Mr. . . .Mr. Conners? Can you hear me?"

Quickly, she put it back to her ear. Through a crackling, she heard his reply. Confidence gained, she spoke again. "Colonel Wadley says, 'Send police.' There's a riot."

Excitedly, she rushed to the door to follow the men. Endine, looking as if her freckles were standing out on stems, blocked her way.

"Where're you going?" Endine shrieked.

"I must see!"

Pushing Endine aside, she stepped out on a wharf filling with men. The work-gnarled faces of the railroad employees held dark-circled eyes quivering with fear.

This was different from the riot she had witnessed in Eufaula. There, men of property, who had been denied the right to vote because of being former Confederate soldiers, had eyes glittering with hatred. They had fought against unscrupulous Northerners who had come south with all they owned in a carpetbag and joined forces with some dishonest southern scalawags. That was political. These men feared hunger.

They were shouting, "How can we feed our children if you cut wages?"

Down the wharf, stevedores stopped unloading a foreign ship and advanced brandishing menacing tools.

Up the riverbank, a group of laborers, several hundred large black men, began marching toward the fray.

Suddenly a scuffle—shots fired—a scream. Was it Endine? The police—the police firing.

Wadley's booming voice shouted above the din. Paul was helping him climb atop a cotton bale.

Colonel Wadley towered over the crowd, a ready target. His thick white hair shining like a crown in the sunlight, his powerful neck in its stiff white collar, his long black coat flapping in the ocean breeze commanded their attention. He lifted both arms skyward, spreading the fingers of his huge blacksmith's hands over the crowd like a benediction.

Silenced, they waited.

"Men, I hazard you all know me, and I know you. I've always been a man of truth in word and action. You have no need for alarm or trouble.

"I see you've heard that firemen and brakemen at the north have struck. One can hardly blame them. Yes, the rumor is true. To finance their rate wars they have cut wages on all who earn more than a dollar a day."

The murmuring swelled into a roar. Again Wadley raised his arms.

"Wait! Wait! I pledge to you justice! I understand your needs! I sympathize! No matter what the northern trunk lines do, the Central Rail Road will have no wage reduction this fall. None before November."

They nudged one another, muttering questioningly.

"I give you my word."

"Colonel Wadley's word is good," came a shout.

"It's good enough for me," said another.

"We'll take you at your word."

Relieved smiles spread over leathery faces as men clapped one another on hard-muscled shoulders and returned to work.

Disaster was averted.

As they returned to the office, Mignonne tucked her hand in Paul's arm. *One day he will become a magnificent knight like Colonel Wadley,* she thought as she gazed at Paul's handsome profile through the eyes of love.

On a peaceful evening a few days later, they returned to the wharf. Mignonne was bubbling with anticipation of the voyage to New York City.

Her feet danced up the gangplank of her first steamship. Tall smokestacks belched black smoke like her little flat-bottomed steamboat, but the new *City of Macon* was a deep-draft, ocean-going ship that was also fitted with towering masts. Sails billowed as they went with the tide down the river's mouth and into the vastness of the Atlantic Ocean.

Paul, amused by her excitement, moved near as she leaned over the rail. He pointed out the stars as, one by one, they began to twinkle.

She licked her lips, savoring the taste of salt from the breeze. Her ears sensed his vibrating voice explaining how the ship navigated by the stars, but her thoughts were swimming helplessly in the romance of the moment; her emotions were quivering with the nearness of this handsome man.

Looking down at her glowing face, her parted lips, Paul took her hand and led her to a spot where, concealed by the sail, they escaped Sarah Lois's watchful eye. No longer laughing at her, he stroked her shining black hair.

"You are the most beautiful girl I have ever seen."

Her lashes fanned back from dark eyes saucy yet clear, innocent yet eager for her first real kiss. She whispered, "Cheri."

He lifted her hands and pressed his mustache into her palms. "It amazes me that you are unspoiled, beautiful without and within."

Suddenly his arms closed roughly around her, and he was kissing her as she had never been kissed before.

The next morning when she went out on deck, Mignonne regretted that she had eaten so many shrimp for supper. The grey ocean rolled, undulated. Waves lifted high, then fell back in white-caps of foam. How different it was from the gentle green Gulf waters of home! There was no land in sight, only waves, only grey sky merging with grey sea so that she could not discern the horizon.

By evening, the rolling was worse. Gales buffeted the ship. Mignonne was disgusted with herself. As much as she longed to be on deck with Paul again, she, whose cradle had been a riverboat, was forced to remain below in her cabin, seasick.

They were four days out in a tropical storm that reached near-hurricane force, but the *City of Macon* endured.

When they docked in New York's harbor, Mignonne quickly forgot her bad moments. The bustling city amazed her. Their carriage rolled along streets crowded with people. Craning her neck at the tall buildings, she wanted to see it all.

The next afternoon they visited the brownstone mansion of William Vanderbilt. Sarah Lois had explained that this was a condolence call because they had not seen him since the death of his father, Cornelius. The two families knew each other from summers spent at fashionable Saratoga Springs.

Colonel Wadley had liked the old Commodore, a ferryman who had also risen from humble beginnings.

Both men had started in railroads when they were independent stretches scattered here and there. They had agreed that railroads should be combined, run from one logical terminal to another, and connect with steamboats. On methods of operation, they disagreed. Wadley had bought or merged railroads. Vanderbilt's acquisitions had been through flamboyant means.

Now, as they paid the formal call, the men's talk turned naturally to railroads. Mignonne realized that Colonel Wadley's tone was exasperated. He also disagreed with William Vanderbilt, who was running the New York Central in a manner profitable only to stockholders.

"But, sir," Colonel Wadley was saying, "don't you eastern fellows care that the rate wars you're fighting for the New York-to-Chicago business are causing chaos? I'm not as concerned about the shock waves you're sending through Wall Street as I am about the workers. The wage cuts are leaving men hungry! We who are strong should bear the infirmities of the weak."

Vanderbilt looked at him arrogantly, and the black whiskers on his jaws shook as he replied, "You sound like that Chicago reporter who asked if I didn't run the railroad for the benefit of the public. As I told him, the public be dammed!"

His wife, Maria, tried to cover the situation with

polite small talk, but the visit quickly ended.

The next morning Endine and Sarah Lois took Mignonne shopping while Colonel Wadley and Rebecca visited Dr. Agnew. Paul disappeared on business of his own.

Walking through the huge stores, Mignonne wished she could be buying a bridal gown and trousseau. Instead, her purchases were a few silk flowers from France and some wide satin ribbon.

Returning to their hotel suite, they had transformed it with displays of their purchases when Rebecca entered alone.

White-lipped, her homely face contorted, her eyes too tear-filled to see their bounty, she told them that spectacles would not help her. The diagnosis, incipient cataract of both eyes, was soothed only in that the cataracts were maturing slowly.

"I apologize for spoiling your trip, girls, but I sent Father to secure passage. I want to go home!"

When Colonel Wadley returned, he was grim. "I'm sorry, my dear. A hurricane—the worst in years, they say—is blocking our way home by sea."

Paul strolled in looking disheveled. His cravat was loosened; his usual self-confidence was missing.

Colonel Wadley turned to him. "Paul, go to the Grand Central Depot and check the situation of traveling by rail. Firemen and brakemen on the Baltimore and Ohio have struck. They received another wage cut. But the sparks for the tinder were

Vanderbilt's arrogant statement quoted in the Chicago *Daily News*. I hazard leaving New York might be difficult—or impossible."

Impossible it proved to be. Although Mignonne sympathized with Miss Rebecca's distress at the enforced stay, she was delighted by time to explore New York City with Paul. Of course, Endine and the alertly chaperoning Sarah Lois accompanied them everywhere. They took her to see the magnificent Metropolitan Museum, and they visited the small art dealer who sold Adrianna Edward's paintings.

They rode about showing her the brownstone mansions and the tenements where half a million men, women, and children lived in such dreadful conditions that Mignonne's stomach turned queasy at the stench. It made her understand what an industrialized society meant. She could see why people living in abject poverty held such resentment for the handful of millionaires who owned railroads, oil refineries, steel and coke mills.

Each day news of strikes worsened. Freight trains, with strikers jobs filled by men too hungry to strike, chugged out of Baltimore. At the junction of Martinsburg, West Virginia, violence exploded. Townspeople joined strikers in chasing police. President Hayes sent federal troops.

Strikes spread along the B & O. In Baltimore, women and children with rocks in hand joined a mob of twenty thousand fighting a bloody skirmish.

Secluded in their hotel suite, the Wadley family read newspaper accounts. The unthinkable happened. The mighty railroads stopped.

Mignonne watched Paul's face as Colonel Wadley read aloud of Pittsburgh's railroad buildings burning in a mass of flames three miles long.

"Buffalo, Boston, Chicago, Providence. The violence has spread. More than a hundred are dead. Millions of dollars of property have burned." The big man sighed deeply. "The strikes have accelerated into a railroad war."

Her lashes lowered as she questioned the far away look on Paul's face. Certainly this was enough to effect him, yet Mignonne realized the source of his tension was something more. Fatuously in love, she imagined that he was struggling with giving up bachelorhood. Of course, she wanted the riots to end, but she reveled in being this close to Paul. If they stayed a little longer, perhaps he would declare his love and ask for her hand in marriage.

As if drawn by her gaze, he came to sit beside her on a deep, soft sofa.

"I've talked Auntie into letting me take you to Delmonico's for dinner tonight," he whispered. "Just the two of us alone."

Her face lit with delight, but his remained slack. He kept a serious tone.

"The time has come when I *must* get back to Georgia. I may have to go on horseback. One way or the other, I must leave."

five

Feeling like a child about to hang up her stocking for Santa Claus, Mignonne took out the special dress she had been saving. It should be perfect for her dinner at Delmonico's with Paul. The exquisite gown belonged to Adrianna. Foy Edward's sophisticated wife had gotten it from the salon of Charles Frederick Worth in Paris.

The white French bunting slipped over Mignonne's head, and she shivered deliciously as it nestled around her delicately boned shoulders. The light, loosely woven fabric was embroidered with pink rosebuds, her favorite flower. A trim of woven silk galloons hung around her arms, and she wondered if the fancy finishing braid would get in her way.

Brushing her dark hair up, she piled it on top of her head and pinned it with pink roses. She stood before the cheval glass and surveyed the results. She looked like a young woman of the world, but she had never sat down with such a large bustle nor walked with such a long train. She took a deep breath. Seeing what that did to the neckline of the dress, she reminded herself not to do it again.

Forcing a self-assured smile, she went out to meet Paul.

He greeted her with elaborate compliments, but

he seemed busy adjusting his silk cravat and would not meet her shining eyes.

When their carriage stopped at the famous Fifth Avenue restaurant, Paul explained that the select few who were socially accepted by Mrs. William Astor entertained here. Upstairs was the ballroom where the Patriarch and Assembly balls were held.

Mignonne's eyes became big and round as they were taken through the ground floor where celebrities came to be seen.

"I think that's Mark Twain," Paul whispered.

Mignonne stumbled over her train.

Oh, dear, she thought, *everyone will think I'm a little girl dressed up in her mother's finery.*

A cold-eyed waiter seated them in a corner of the downstairs café. Mignonne confessed to Paul that she felt intimidated. "Since we've been at the North, several clerks have laughed when I asked to buy something. They sneer at the way I talk and say, 'What part of the South are you all from, honey?'"

"What do you reply?"

"I just smile and say, 'The very best part.' I'd never be so rude as to tell them that 'you all' means more than one person or that *their* accent sounds funny to me."

Paul laughed, but he saved her further embarrassment by ordering for her. She had never heard of many items on the menu.

Usually attentive and romantic, Paul fiddled nervously with the silverware while his eyes roamed the café. Leaning back from her, he began to talk about the riots.

"The strikes have spread to the West. There's trouble at Louisville and Galveston. In San Francisco, police arrested men throwing bottles of benzine, burning houses of Chinese, turning railroad trouble into riots against race."

"How terrible," she murmured. *Terrible, yes, but not close enough to cause this change in him.* Crumbling a bit of bread, she peeped up at him through her dark fringe of bangs.

He said nothing more.

Laughing as lightly as possible, she changed the subject. With her voice honeyed and her smile flirtatious, she said, "I'm surprised that Miss Sarah Lois let us come alone. Endine was so angry that she clamped her teeth together and didn't say one mumbling word when she buttoned up the back of my dress."

She took a deep breath, waited.

His reply was flat. "Auntie knew I had to talk with you before I left."

"You're still going? How can you travel with the riots worse?"

"Someway." He shrugged. "I must."

"Oh." It was a small sound.

He closed his hand over her agitated fingers clutching the bread, "I've got to make you understand. I'd hoped. . . .You see, I overheard Cousin William saying something important. I thought I'd make a fortune on the stock market. But when things didn't go as he expected, he changed plans." He sighed heavily. "I didn't know that so I lost everything."

"Cheri, money doesn't matter. . ."

She stopped short and her dark, liquid eyes widened as he handed her a small, square box.

She ripped off the wrapping. Disappointment slid over her face.

"Just a trinket," he said. From the box that was shaking in her hand, he lifted a small cameo set on a carnelian. "So you won't forget our fun in New York."

She touched the cold red stone. "I'll never, never forget!"

She pressed her lips together to stop her chin from quivering. Ducking her head to hide her tear-filled eyes from him, she pinned the cameo at the neck of her dress. She hoped he would not guess she had expected the box to contain an engagement ring.

He cleared his throat. "I leave tomorrow. Regardless. To be back in time for the wedding."

"Wedding! Whose wedding?"

"Mine."

She felt her mouth open, her throat constrict. She could not speak.

"You don't know? Didn't Endine tell you about Victoria?"

She shook her head so violently that her hair began to slip down her neck.

"When we were children, our families planned we should marry. They still believe in combining plantations and keeping blood blue. My mother has a pedigree, but my father doesn't have the money. The Landinghams are the richest folks in the county. They live in a castle-like house built on a

foundation of ballast stones brought on ships—
'From the *old* country,'" he mimicked. "Victoria
acts as if she were her namesake. We've been en-
gaged forever. I postponed our marriage once. Now
I must. . ."

The waiter stood at Mignonne's elbow with a rich
dessert. She shook her head and pressed her fingers over her mouth. Her stomach flip-flopped at
the thought of whipped cream.

Somehow she held herself erect and managed her
train correctly when she walked past Mark Twain.
She endured the carriage ride around Central Park.
But when they stood alone in the dim hotel corridor, the French endearments from the tender moments of her childhood slipped out unbidden.

"Oh, Paul! Je t'aime!"

Her cheeks flaming, her hair tumbling, she
whirled and fled into her room. In the darkness,
she leaned weakly against the door.

Endine's breathing was undisturbed. Asleep.
Thank goodness!

Struggling with the tiny covered buttons down
her back, Mignonne flung off the sophisticated finery. Creeping into her bed in her corset and petti-
coat, she let silent tears slip down her cheeks.

She wished she could wake Endine and shake
her 'til her freckles fell off. *Why didn't she warn
me about Victoria, the richest girl in the county?*

Queen Victoria. Endine did warn her! But cryp-
tically. And Sarah Lois. That dear old maid had
kept her carefully chaperoned. Then, she let them
be alone when this shame was revealed. *She kept*

me from making an utter fool...

Endine might hear, but Mignonne could no longer hold back sobs.

Paul left on a Pennsylvania train that secured its way down the track by pushing a gondola car mounted with a squad of soldiers and a Gatling gun.

Through miserable days, Mignonne, tasting pain and understanding Rebecca's need, wanted only to go home.

William Wadley paced their small parlor. The situation demanded his presence back in Georgia. The tender heart of the big, gruff man would not let him leave his wife who was in despair at the prospect of blindness.

Mail trains, always slow at best, were not crossing the strike zone. By telegraph, Wadley learned that the strike fever had not spread to the South. In Georgia, the Central's timetables were intact.

Mignonne telegraphed her parents that she was safe.

Endine fretted about the mail. Her letters were not getting through to Zachary.

At last a milk train brought them a copy of the Savannah *Morning News*.

Eagerly, Colonel Wadley read to them, "The people generally in this section are on strike—at mosquitoes and flies. Prickly heat is the prevailing complaint. These fine evenings, lovers sit on stoops to conquer."

Laughing at the pun, Sarah Lois said, "I hope he isn't overconfident."

"Do you think our workmen will continue to decline engaging in this terrible bloodshed?" asked Rebecca.

"I pray they will," he replied. "In the North, industrial men out of work are a drain. But we are agricultural. The hard school the South has been through has taught self-reliance. We can still eat even if we must tighten our belts. We can stand panics, failure, depression, war. We can live within ourselves."

Mignonne, sunk into the sofa, lifted her pale face to look at him. She smiled. It was funny that his self-inclusive speech was delivered in a crisp, New Hampshire twang, but it reminded her of her heritage.

She stiffened her spine. Hadn't her parents taught her to be gracious in the face of adversity, to rely on God to lift her above the storm? She would not let them see her cry.

Finally, the hurricane passed. They returned to Savannah by ship. The seas were still tempestuous, but less so than the railroads.

She must not think how different Colonel Wadley's word was from Paul's. She must only be thankful that his workmen had trusted him and had kept Georgia railroads running. She sped back across the state, up the red sand hills to the bluff of her beloved Chattahoochee, across the trestle, into Alabama.

Eufaula. Home!

Throwing herself into her mother's arms, she wept.

six

Lily Wingate stroked Mignonne's black hair, holding her close, letting her cry. When it became apparent that the tears were unceasing, she led her upstairs to the privacy of her pink-and-white bedroom.

"Oh, Mama," Mignonne wailed, "I thought 'cause I loved all them, they should love me. Endine turned so mean. So secretive and—" Realization surprised her. "And jealous! And Paul. . ." Her voice trembled over sobs. "Oh, Mama, I was *sure* he loved me. But . . .he. . .he's going to m. . .m. . .marry Queen Victoria!"

Lily's lively face fell slack. Then her brown eyes twinkled. "I'm quite sure the old lady won't have him."

A giggle, near to hysteria, squeaked through Mignonne's snuffling, but she calmed and explained about the Landinghams.

"How well I understand!" Her mother said. "Your grandmother had everything arranged for me to marry Green Bethune. She meant to bind the ties with the aristocratic part of the family in South Carolina. I felt I had to do my duty and obey my parents."

"But you got out of it."

"Not before I spent a lot of time in helpless,

hopeless weeping. But that was before I began to read my Bible and pray for guidance."

A big tear rolled down Mignonne's cheek. Lily wiped it with her forefinger. Then she gently cuffed Mignonne's elfin-pointed chin, tilting it upward. She was smiling tenderly, but Mignonne shielded herself from the probing gaze with lashes thick with tears.

"You are so loved here at home that it's hard to find out everyone doesn't love you. Especially when you have so much love to give. But, darling, don't rush headlong through life and miss the joys of being young."

Mignonne frowned and pulled away.

Lily continued talking quietly. "Marriage was God's first institution. We each should pray for Him to lead us to the one He has chosen for us to marry. Only with a marriage founded on God's love can we truly be one in mind and spirit—as well as body . . . I know how handsome, how exciting Paul was. Of course, you were infatuated but—"

"No, Mama. I *love* Paul!"

Lily nodded. "And now you're exhausted from your journey. But you'll feel better after you've had your cry and a good long rest."

She turned back the snowy counterpane on the high rosewood bed, the same bed that had once received her tears. Slender posts, rising high over their heads, supported a graceful curved frame draped now for Mignonne in white organdy caught with pink ribbons.

Wearily, Mignonne climbed on the stool and sank

into the comfort of the feather bed as her mother gently closed the door.

I'm grown up enough to be in love, she thought. *Mama doesn't understand.* She was determined to sort through her problems, but her fingers automatically found the frayed knots of candlewicking on the ancient counterpane. Rubbing them in the old familiar way, she fell asleep.

Morning dawned so brightly it was difficult to maintain melancholy. Mignonne set to work letting out the tucks in the embroidered bunting that had made the statuesque Adrianna's dress fit her small frame. Suddenly, the scene at Delmonico's was all too vivid, making her bite her lip until the taste of blood was added to her salty tears. She heated a smoothing iron in the fireplace. Carefully pressing the dress, she folded it with tissue into a tremendous box.

She hitched a mare to the phaeton. Balancing the box beside her on the seat of the small cart, she drove slowly along the wide boulevard of Eufaula Avenue. Sheltering trees rustled overhead. A yellow leaf fell into her lap. She fancied it saying, *welcome home.*

Mignonne looked about as if seeing the peaceful scene for the first time. She had taken living in Eufaula for granted. Along this street, one mansion stood staunchly beside another. Towering Italianate structures topped by belvederes and widows' walks smiled down upon square, solid Greek Revival edifices with round, white columns. They shared the street with a few new houses sporting modern gingerbread trim.

As she passed, people waved at her from cool, shady porches and bright, blossoming gardens.

Yes, it was good to be home where everyone knew and loved her.

Or did they? Did they think her spoiled? Self-centered? What had she ever done to deserve their love?

They had reached Barbour Street. "Gee!" she said to old Minnie who obediently turned right.

They climbed the hill. Past Cato's. She should visit. There, crowning the crest, stood Barbour Hall. Funny. She had never realized its magnificence.

Constructed in her grandmother's day in 1854, it had been white with green shutters. Now—to the consternation of everyone in town—Adrianna had painted it in shades of brown. Her artist's eye had brought out the splendid architectural details of the Italianate mansion. The tremendous porch, which skirted the front and both sides, was trimmed with slender brown columns set in pairs and interspersed with cream-colored scrollwork arches. Chocolate brown shutters framed the floor-to-ceiling windows. Contrasting trim continued on the second story and high atop the roof on the balustrade surrounding the multi-windowed belvedere.

Driving past the red cedars at the gate, Mignonne tied the horse to the hitching post and wrestled the box up the steep steps. Barbour Hall was built high off the ground, and she had played house in the damp coolness beneath it when her doting grandmother, Cordelia Edwards, was alive.

The double doorway, surrounded by glass side-lights, always had a welcoming look. She knocked and then let herself into the marble-floored hall calling, "Adrianna."

The elegantly tall girl emerged from the back room. Mignonne felt comfortable knowing she would never encounter jealousy from Adrianna. She had red hair, but unlike Endine's mousy friz, hers was a dazzling cascade of red-gold. With her apple-cheeked smile, Adrianna was stunningly beautiful. Being a matron of twenty-one, she traveled in a different social circle, but Mignonne knew she was a true friend.

Foy came out to greet her. Nestled in the crook of his elbow was two-month-old Foy Edwards, Junior.

"Ohhh, he's grown!" Mignonne exclaimed. Her arms, aching with yearning, reached out for him. Cuddling him to her breast, she kissed his fuzzy halo of red-gold hair.

Foy explained he had merely left his cotton factor's office for a moment to get a bite to eat.

Mignonne watched them standing over her with their heads close together cooing to the baby. She knew food was an excuse to come home. Their obvious love made tears rush to the surface. She returned the baby.

"Go on with your snack. I'll tell you about New York later. I need some time alone. . .to think. I'd like to sit awhile in the belvedere, if I may?"

"Of course. For as long as you like," replied Adrianna quickly.

Turning away, Mignonne climbed the flights of stairs unseeingly. Her friend's understanding had been too quick. Did everyone know about Paul? *How embarrassing,* she thought as she emerged from the dark attic into the sun-drenched glassed tower.

Crowning the steep roof of the tall house, the belvedere had been built for ventilation. With its windows open, hot air rising from the central hall escaped here, cooling the house. Clare Edwards had also used the belvedere for weather observation, but his children had considered it a sanctuary.

Now, Mignonne breathed deeply, seeking the peace her mother had found here. She stepped out on the porch-like widow's walk. Her knuckles white, she grasped the balustrade.

Uhmmm! Uhmmmmm!

The steamboat's whistle quickened her heartbeat, drew her gaze down the Chattahoochee. Puffs of smoke rising above the trees marked the path of the steamer carrying cotton to Appalachicola Bay. Longing seized her, to be aboard it, to be going somewhere, anywhere. The embarrassment of sympathetic eyes was worse than losing Paul.

Struggling to calm herself, she stood a long while. Then she remembered her mother's admonition to pray.

With the sweet voice of a little child, Mignonne implored, "Dear God, please make Paul love me."

In the weeks that passed, Mignonne found an excuse to visit the post office after each mail train.

No letter came. None from Endine. None from Paul. No apology. No explanation for allowing her to think he loved her.

She imagined scenes in which Paul jilted Victoria and came to claim her. A letter arrived. She ripped it open.

Endine's scrawl went on for pages telling how Zachary had not understood why he received no letters from New York and had found someone else. A brief note on the back of a page told about Paul's wedding. Endine ended by pleading to come to Eufaula for a visit. Mignonne ignored the request.

Winter stretched ahead of her, long, lonely, wet, gray.

Christmas busied her hands with preparing gifts, baking, decorating her mother's home. Then she had nothing to do.

She had finished her education at the local academy. How she wished that she could go to Philadelphia to finishing school! She could not ask. After having been away and having seen stylish people, she realized Mama and Papa still wore clothes from before the war. She knew it was because they lacked money for better.

She wished that she could work, but the jobs that women had filled during the war were once again deemed unsuitable now that men had returned to do them. It was considered highly improper for a lady to work.

There was only marriage.

Months passed. Mignonne attended teas and showers and weddings as one by one her friends married. There were fewer and fewer beaus left to squire her to the Volunteer Firemen's drills and balls. She was rapadly becoming an old maid.

On a sweltering July day, Endine appeared at the door unannounced. She had accompanied Colonel Wadley, who had come to buy the Montgomery and Eufaula Railroad.

The funny girl had not altered by one freckle, but when the Wadley family arrived for a hurriedly arranged dinner party, it was apparent that they had changed. Miss Rebecca was barely able to see, and Colonel Wadley was ill. The big man seemed to struggle for breath in the thick, humid air.

After the meal, when the men had sought the breeze on the corner of the porch, Sarah Lois explained how sick he had been.

"Dr. Flewellen has discovered symptoms of disease of the heart. He suggests a change of climate and taking the mineral waters of Saratoga Springs, New York. We are leaving soon.

"Mignonne, would you like to go to the Adirondack Mountains with us?"

"Please, please say you'll go!" Endine's yellow eyes gleamed.

Mignonne's accepting heart thought her sincere. Restlessness overcoming judgement, she said, "Yes!"

seven

Eyes shining, lavender-kid-gloved hands clasped in delight, Mignonne stood amidst her pile of trunks, bandboxes, and hat boxes. A kaleidoscope of colorfully dressed travelers patterned and repatterned the train station platform. At other depots on the long journey, somber people had moved with businesslike directness. Here in the resort town of Saratoga, New York, cheery greetings filled the air. Everyone moved with the sense that something pleasant was about to happen.

The arriving families of the millionaires—bankers, politicians, and especially railroad men—were elaborately dressed in spite of the smut and cinders and steam escaping around them. The ladies' gowns of rich materials had pleated underskirts with overskirts draped like aprons in front and pulled back into bustles that cascaded into trains, dragging behind, dusting the platform.

Townspeople in working clothes, summoned by the tolling bells and blasting whistles, stood at the side murmuring in awe as they identified the Vanderbilts and Dom Pedro, Emperor of Brazil.

Mignonne, gazing in wonderment, was unaware that many of the eyes were watching her. Her simple gray serge traveling costume and lavender-ribboned hat could not conceal her vitality, her bloom of youth.

Sarah Lois beckoned from across the crowd. She threaded her way to where the Wadleys were boarding an omnibus. Directing the red-capped porter about her baggage, she kept her jewel case on the seat beside her. It held her mother's emeralds and Aunt Emma's precious rubies.

"I wish Mama could see this greenness!" she exclaimed as the omnibus swayed along the elm-lined street. "It even smells green!"

White houses—did they all have fresh paint and gingerbread trim?—were set in smooth green lawns. Back home by August, sparse grass and drooping flowers were parched by heat and drought; corn fields were turning brown for harvest. Here geraniums were vivid, lawns were lush.

Sniffing the pine-scented air, she held onto her hat as she tilted back her head to see the tops of the evergreen mountains ringing the small town.

They passed amazing hotels. The tremendous United States Hotel had six or seven stories. The high arches over the porch rose above the fourth floor.

"Here they call a porch a piazza," Endine told her. "That one is the Grand Union Hotel owned by Judge Henry Hilton. It's considered Saratoga's masterpiece."

Mignonne preferred the Clarendon House. Pure white with green shutters, it had a simple portico with towering round columns that reminded her of houses back home.

But they kept going. They stopped at last at Congress Hall.

"It overlooks the best of the springs," Endine explained. "Drinking the Congress water has helped Cousin William before."

Nestled amid pines, Congress Hall was surrounded by spreading lawns where white-suited guests were playing croquet and the new rage, lawn tennis.

They crossed the long piazza, which was filled with rocking-chaired guests who paused mid-rock but did not speak. Stepping into the walnut-paneled lobby, Mignonne paused. The room had a dark, rich elegance, but it was hard to see in the dim yellow gaslight. The blur of impatient humanity seemed all noise and movement as loud-voiced guests checked in and bellhops scurried. Leaning back in the shadows, she closed her eyes wearily.

When she lifted her fan of lashes, her eyes were drawn to a young man in a quiet corner beyond the melee.

He stood, feet apart, hands relaxed. He had thick, straight brows that hooded deep-set eyes directed away from her. He was looking out a side door as if he drew his calmness from somewhere far away.

Surprising herself, Mignonne noticed how soft his mustache looked, not waxed and twirled, but small, neat, revealing the firm line of his lips. She smiled because he had not followed the dictates of this be whiskered generation. There were no muttonchop whiskers hiding his strong jawline. Something about his clean cheek made her want to reach out, to touch it. Tenderness swelled up, warming her face.

Drawing her breath with alarm lest he catch her gazing in such an unladylike manner, she tried to pull her eyes away.

He moved.

She drew back behind a velvet drapery, unable to stop watching.

He knelt beside a wheelchair. His hands moved quietly. Big, strong, yet gentle, they tucked a lap robe around a fretful old man. He said words she could not hear and stood again, unfolding long legs. She had not realized he was so tall! She leaned forward, drawn from the protecting shadows.

At that moment, a dazzling young woman with hair of spun gold swished through the middle of the lobby. Behind her beribboned train came a maid carrying a parrot in a gilded cage; a footman with a lapdog under each arm; and the full retinue of tall black bellhops bearing sixteen Saratoga trunks on backs, twenty-five bandboxes under arms, and seven hat boxes balanced on heads.

Mignonne gaped at the amazing procession. When it had passed, he was gone. Endine's elbow in her ribs made her turn and follow into the wrought-iron cage of the elevator.

In the room they shared, Mignonne carefully unpacked her clothes. She could not compete with that blond—five of the woman's trunks were coffin-like oblongs that, undoubtedly, contained ball gowns—but Mignonne was satisfied with her wardrobe, which everyone at home had helped to prepare for the visit to the famous resort.

Smiling, she remembered her mother's voice repeating the adage, "A lady is known by her silks and velvets."

Gaily, Lily had ripped apart her pre-war hooped skirts, which yielded yards and yards of fine material. Adrianna had arrived with her latest issues of *Harper's Bazar* and her artist's pencils to design for Mignonne. Emma came with needles and thread. Kitty, who had been with the family for so long that she was part of it, carefully mended and washed and ironed Grandmother Cordelia's exquisite European laces. Adrianna had shown Mignonne how she could change the look of her garments with additions of lace collars and shawls.

Now, as she placed the clothing in a huge walnut armoire, Mignonne repeated her mother's words, "Don't worry; be yourself."

Amazed that they had their own private bathroom with a walnut-boxed tub, she took off the many layers of confining undergarments and sank into warm, soapy water. It felt good to soak away the grime from the long, slow trip.

They had crossed Georgia in Colonel Wadley's private car. For some reason, he had stopped at every bridge and intersection, inspecting, talking with employees, making notes of suggestions and complaints.

The sea voyage from Savannah had made her cheeks burn with the memory of Paul's kisses. How glad she was that she had been careful to restrain him! Her feelings of betrayal had made her vow not to give her heart so easily again.

In New York City, Colonel Wadley had become alarmingly ill. Dr. Clark diagnosed dropsy of the chest. His treatment brought improvement after a few days, and they continued the journey to Colonel Wadley's old homestead, Great Hill, near Brentwood, New Hampshire.

They had left Exeter, New Hampshire, that morning, the first day of August, and arrived, at last, in this beautiful mountain retreat. She was lucky to be included. Most folks never left the county in which they were born. Only the wealthy traveled.

Refreshed from her bath, she discovered as she dressed for dinner that she was famished.

The older Wadleys were too tired to leave their rooms, but Sarah Lois, knowing the girls' excitement, agreed to chaperone them in the dining room.

Mignonne's healthy appetite was put to the test by course after course of elaborate food. She delighted in her first taste of such local delicacies as brook trout.

"There'll be a hop tonight," Endine told her as they dipped into a dessert of raspberries and cream.

"A hop?"

"Don't you know anything? A dance. Informal. In the garden."

"But. . ." She looked around the crowded dining

room. "We don't know a soul. We couldn't dance with anyone without being properly introduced."

"That's why I wanted you along." Endine laughed with glee. "Last year I had a terrible time. These nouveau riche snobs won't let many southerners into their exclusive 'four hundred.'"

"I wouldn't feel too slighted, dear," Sarah Lois said with a twinkle in her dark eyes. "Caroline Astor doesn't even acknowledge the Vanderbilts."

"We'll have fun anyway, Endine," Mignonne said soothingly. "But we can't go to the cotillion—hop—without escorts."

"Oh, we'll have 'em! I took out insurance for that: your black velvet hair, milk-white skin, and flirty brown eyes." She shrugged unconcernedly. "You'll draw a crowd. And—"

"I don't flirt!"

"Yes, you do, my little magnolia blossom. You clap those little hands together in delight—and you say exactly what you mean."

"Huh?"

"You don't even know enough about sophisticated courting to say vague things that keep 'em guessing." Endine wrinkled her freckled nose. "But! When the bees swarm around you, some of them will have sense enough to notice that I have a better figure—and a better wit."

Before Mignonne could form a reply, Endine punched her ribs and shushed her.

A short, round woman from three tables over had gotten up and was bearing down upon them.

Apparently, she always ate every bite of every course. Her tightly stretched, lavishly tasseled gown made her look like an overstuffed chair pulling window drapes for a train.

"Miss Wadley," the chair said loudly. "How nice to see you again! May I introduce my nephew, G. Warren Smith of New York, and Richard Chittenden, son of Representative Chittenden of Brooklyn."

Mignonne suppressed a giggle. The young men in the chair's wake were trying to look worldly while struggling to avoid stepping on her train.

Both were dressed in linen suits with windowpane cheeks. They sported large mustaches and looked as if they spent a great deal of time waxing them and twirling up the corners. The muttonchops of one were pale blond, while the other's were black. She did not know which man was which.

It amazed her that she was dressed well enough for these dandies to desire an introduction. But, of course, she was wearing Aunt Emma's necklace of pink rubies.

Swallowing her mirth and her doubts, Mignonne graciously acknowledged the introductions and allowed Mr. Smith to escort her to the hop held in the enclosed garden behind the hotel.

Endine triumphantly swung on Chittenden's arm and disappeared into the shadows cast by Chinese lanterns strung among the trees.

The orchestra was playing music unfamiliar to Mignonne, but Mr. Smith assured her he could teach her the dance. As she stumbled through the intricate figures of the German, she protested that all eyes were upon her.

Mr. Smith laughed and confirmed that indeed they were. "But it's because an impromptu vote has proclaimed you the most beautiful girl at the Congress. They all want to teach you to dance."

She smiled politely. He really was quite nice, but somehow as they whirled through the intermingling waltzes, her eyes, of their own volition, searched the garden for the quiet young man.

Why did I notice him? she wondered wistfully. *He really wasn't handsome like Paul.*

The next morning, not knowing what was involved in "taking the waters" but being warned by Endine that all of Saratoga would turn out to see and be seen, Mignonne chose her favorite morning outfit. The fine old India muslin had been boiled in the wash pot by Kitty until it sparkled purest white. Emma had cut the sheer material into endless puffs and sewn it together with Cordelia's Valenciennes lace. Beneath this airy confection was a pink silk underskirt, tightly fitted down to Mignonne's little kid slippers.

To keep the dress sweet and simple, they had not used a bustle and train. Instead, wide pink ribbon formed a sash Mignonne tied into a series of complicated knots that cascaded down the back of the skirt ending in streamers.

She pinned on the hat that Adrianna had made,

using only three pink rosebuds and a few bits of
lace. Donning the short tunic of pink silk bordered
with lace, she pulled on her gloves and turned, ready
to go.

Endine still stood in pantaloons and corset.
"You'll never catch a millionaire looking that sweet
and innocent," she said sourly.

"I didn't come to catch a millionaire."

"I did."

"Endine!"

"What better place? The American Bankers'
Association convenes here today—tighten my
corset."

"You can't breathe now," Mignonne protested.
But she obediently pulled and tugged at the corset's
strings until it pushed up Endine's bosom and
cinched in her waist.

Red-faced, Endine gasped and frowned at
Mignonne. "You really should have been nicer to
Mr. Smith. He's the most eligible bachelor here."

"But—"

"You don't appreciate how lucky you were to be
introduced. Proper introductions are more than just
required good manners here. They're insurance.
Why, you wouldn't believe how many fortune hunters who pretend to be something they are not come
here. Sometimes they are able to fool folks with
their charm and marry into money."

Mignonne waited in silence while Endine dressed
in an elaborate gown. It was laden with costly trims
on a bustle so large that when she put on a

long-billed hat, she looked exactly like a red-headed goose waddling along twitching its tail feathers.

Suppressing a laugh, Mignonne thought that Endine would surely attract attention. She wondered why she did not class herself a fortune hunter.

No millionaire hunting for me, she thought. *I've had quite enough of men who place money before love or honor.*

The crisp morning air was delicious to Mignonne as she followed Colonel Wadley, Miss Rebecca, and Miss Sarah Lois along the walkway to the spring. They assured her the waters of the Congress were superior to all of the springs of Saratoga.

Lagging behind, Endine struggled along the broken brick sidewalk in French heels two inches high.

Mignonne, drinking in the beauty of her surroundings, let her gaze wander up the green mountainsides. Humming merrily as she strolled along, she twirled her white-ruffled parasol over her shoulder. The pink silk lining cast a rosy glow over her lovely face. Her loosely brushed hair bounced around her shoulders, and the streamers of her sash floated behind as she walked.

The pathway curved, and she brought her eyes back to earth. The Wadleys had disappeared around a stand of shrubs. She drew in her breath.

The young man stood in the middle of the walkway. He had ceased his struggle to push the wheelchair over the rough pavement and was standing, looking at her with his face full of wonder.

Lowering her long lashes demurely, Mignonne could not resist a glimpse through the roses of the hat that tilted provocatively over her bangs.

He had sandy hair. It tried to escape its neat combing and spring into curls.

Her lips twitched to suppress a smile. Propriety did not allow her to speak. It decreed that she must discreetly lower the pink parasol.

That done, she could only see his legs, long in a tan-striped seersucker morning suit. But she could see the man in the invalid chair. Straight brows over deep-set eyes and a fringe of sandy curls around his balding head made it obvious that he was the father, but his face was furrowed with such pain that she had to give him her most encouraging smile.

He smiled back, relaxing stiff shoulders.

"Good morning." She dropped a slight curtsy and fled to catch the Wadleys. They were already going down the wooden steps of the planking that boxed in the spring.

They sat down and waited. Young boys with cups attached to long sticks dipped them into the opening. They hurried to the waiting ladies and gentlemen who tipped them. A few people seemed to enjoy the water, but most drank with wry faces.

Mignonne sipped carefully. Quickly, she covered her mouth with her handkerchief. Having no rheumatism or diarrhea or any of the various complaints said to be cured by the waters, she surreptitiously poured the bitter stuff on a petunia bed.

The rest of the morning was spent on the piazza

where Colonel Wadley conversed with old cronies. Few came from the South since the war, but those few were drawn to Colonel Wadley.

While the older folks took an afternoon nap, Mignonne found a copy of Mark Twain's book *The Adventures of Tom Sawyer.* Having seen the author, she could hardly wait to read his popular novel.

In the cool of early evening, Colonel Wadley hired a barouche, and they joined the parade of carts and carriages driving up and down Broadway. The girls leaned out, longing for a closer look at the wares on the tables set up along the street. Their driver did not stop.

At that evening's hop, so many young men had availed themselves of the services of Mrs. "Chair" that Mignonne's dance card was completely filled by the time the old woman announced loudly that she was going to bed.

At ten-thirty, a breathless Mignonne was drinking punch when she saw him. He stepped into the far end of the garden. Their eyes met in quiet communion across the wildly gyrating dancers.

It was childish for her to imagine that the music swelled. She must not let herself become infatuated as she had with Paul. She did not want to be betrayed again. She broke the spell of his gaze and looked away.

Curiosity made her peep over her cup. He was waving his arms ridiculously. Obviously, he was arguing with Mr. Smith. Then he approached Mr. Chittenden, who looked toward her and shook his head. She wondered what was going on.

As she was whirled around the garden, she kept seeing him pleading with first one and then the other of the young men who had signed her dance card.

When the closing song began, she glimpsed his disappointed face and realized his problem. He could find no one who would introduce them.

eight

Rain slid down the wavery glass of the bedroom window. Mignonne looked out expecting to see the beautiful circle of mountains. Instead, clouds lowered over the small lake, concealing the surrounding slopes, shutting her in. Even the swans and ducks had disappeared into the sheltering hemlocks.

Disappointed, she shivered and dug into her trunk for a warm cashmere shawl. She had protested when Emma had packed it. Now she was glad for her wisdom. She had never been this cold in August.

Usually she enjoyed a rainy day as an excuse to do nothing but read. Now she fretted. How awful to waste a day of their visit, which was all too brief.

With nothing else to do, the girls stayed in their room. With a *Harper's Bazar* to guide her and a curling iron heated in the fireplace, Mignonne practiced with Endine's red hair. Already kinking from the dampness, it rolled easily into a myriad of long curls. She piled them upon the crown of Endine's head and arranged them down the back of her neck in the high fashion style.

Her own hair, heavy and lank from the rain, refused to curl. Pouting at her reflection, she could only brush it into shining smoothness.

That afternoon, declaring her hairstyle too gorgeous to remain hidden behind closed doors, Endine dragged Mignonne out into the rain. It had been announced that the famous Miss Sarah Smiley was to give a Bible lesson. They joined a group bundling into carriages bound for the Grand Union Hotel.

Mignonne was surprised at the throng of gaily dressed people. They crowded the adjoining saloons to hear the sweet-looking woman in her simple dark gown and bonnet. What a diverse group! She recognized the vice-president of the country. Next to him was a banker well-known for swindles and crookedness. Were these people sinners seeking salvation or hypocrites with nothing else to do? She could not tell.

Covertly, she eyed the group of elegant young men standing in the doorways. They were pulling out pocket Bibles, following Miss Smiley's reading of texts, looking innocent and wholesome. *He* was not in the group.

He gave up on meeting me rather easily, she thought, making a sour mouth. Remembering how her grandmother had suffered on rainy days, she figured he must have stayed in to nurse his father. *The dutiful son.*

Probably I imagined that he was interested in me just because I thought he looked special.

She wiped tears, telling herself they were caused by fumes from the fireplaces. She hated smelly sham fires of gas instead of clean-smelling wood.

Still feeing cross when they returned to the Congress, Mignonne had sudden pangs of conscience. She had not listened to a word of the Scripture.

A note from Sarah Lois told them to dress for a dinner party to be hosted by Colonel Wadley. Wet, cold, not wanting to dress again, Mignonne decided to stay in the room. She had become engrossed in *The Adventures of Tom Sawyer.* Sometimes Mama scolded her for being anti-social and retreating into her own world of books, but she decided to plead a headache.

The private dining hall was drafty. Colonel Wadley had a blanket shawl draped about his massive shoulders as he received his guests. William Vanderbilt, his wife, and their young daughter (who had been declared the most beautiful girl at the hop at the United States Hotel the evening before) had already arrived when Mignonne walked into the room.

She was surprised that Colonel Wadley noticed her. He nodded and beamed approval. She was glad that she had reconsidered rejecting his invitation, glad that she had worn her best dinner dress of green velvet. Elegantly cut, it had a portrait neckline. Framing her face were Lily's emerald necklace and earrings.

She was introduced to old Judge Jewell of the Alabama Claims' Commission. He asked about her family and offered his arm to escort her to the table. Assuming the old man from back home was the reason for her invitation, she was about to be seated between him and the Reverend Dr. McGoon, a minister from Philadelphia, when with a squeak of wheels, the last guests arrived.

Colonel Wadley summoned her. "Mignonne, may I present my old friend, Colonel Francis Edgefield. He has a fine old rice plantation on the Combahee River in the low country of South Carolina. But he was also in on the beginning of railroading with the Best Friend of Charleston about the time I went to Savannah."

"How do you do, Mignonne," he said in a weak voice. He spoke haltingly because his teeth were too large for a face once-round, now hollowed by illness.

Mignonne curtsied and spoke graciously, but her hands were suddenly wet, her skin was prickling. Her satin-lined mantilla slipped from her bare shoulders and slid to the floor. *However will I retrieve it gracefully?* she wondered, not daring to breathe.

Colonel Wadley was ignoring the tall man holding the wheel chair. He continued speaking to Francis Edgefield.

"Mignonne is the daughter of Captain Harrison Wingate—you know, of the Wingate Steamboat Line out of Demopolis, Alabama. Her mother is the daughter of Clare Edwards, late cotton factor of Eufaula."

Wondering why he was giving her pedigree as if they were still in the deep South, she nodded politely. Then, unable to help herself, she looked up at the handsome young man.

His hands rested quietly on the handles of the chair, but he was leaning forward, his smooth lean cheeks shining with eagerness.

Colonel Wadley chuckled. As if it were an afterthought, he added, "Oh, yes, this is his youngest son, Robert Edgefield."

Pleased that she was able to maintain her poise in spite of the fact that her heart and lungs were forgetting to function, Mignonne extended her hand.

Robert clicked his heels together and bowed to kiss her hand, somehow combining formal correctness with casual grace.

"I've been wanting to meet you, Miss Wingate," Robert said in a cultured South Carolina voice. It was warm, deep for so young a man.

"Yes, I saw. . ." She caught her lip in her teeth and grinned impishly. Endine's scorn for her speaking her mind echoed a warning.

Robert's candid blue eyes twinkled. He had caught her meaning. Understanding passed between them.

He bent to pick up her shawl. Rubbing the smooth satin in his fingers for a moment, he considered. Then, as if the gesture were ever so casual, he spread it behind her and placed it gently on both shoulders.

A blush rose from deep within her as if she were a rosebud unfurling into a full-blown blossom.

"I really don't need it," she stammered. "It's *quite* warm in here."

Dinner was announced, and she was seated

between the old gentlemen. Robert was on the opposite side of the table.

They could only steal glances, not knowing what to say.

For the soup course, a bowl covered with bread and sealed with melted cheese was set before Mignonne. *However do I eat it?* she wondered. Dipping in her spoon, she lifted cheese, stringing from the bowl to her mouth, wrapping around her chin.

Robert chuckled and twirled his cheese around his spoon. "It's hard to eat, but it's worth it."

Digging deeper, she savored the hot, brown soup. "Wonderful," she agreed. "Especially after a day of being wet."

Suddenly Robert seemed as comfortable to her as a favorite reading chair.

"You don't know how nice it is to talk with some one who drawls as much as I do," she said, laughing. "People here are too polite to make fun of you, but—and this is almost worse—they stifle thought by commanding, 'Say something else. We love to hear you talk.'"

Like old friends, they discussed the book she was reading. They agreed that Mark Twain's saga had caught the simplicity of pre-Civil War life, an innocence now gone.

They were perfectly happy that the meal lasted for hours. Course after course was served. Plates were removed, and more food was placed before them. Mignonne tasted succulent trout, nibbled savory game, wondered at exotic vegetables, identified only the corn on the cob.

Occasionally she chatted with the old gentlemen on either side of her. Always she could feel the warmth of Robert's gaze upon her, appreciative yet undemanding.

She avoided looking at Endine, who cackled a faked laugh from the other end of the table. She was after her latest conquest, a count.

Suddenly Judge Jewell's voice boomed over the individual conversations. "I commend you, Colonel Wadley, for taking your fight with General Alexander to the courts. It is obvious to all that he's being used by that Wall Street syndicate to gain control of the Central."

"He's schemed to split my board of directors and temporarily inflate the stock," Wadley explained. His big fist slammed down on the table flipping a fork. "I refuse to consent to payment of dividends not earned."

Francis Edgefield's weak voice joined in. "With northern and western railroads failing and going into receivership, it's nearly unbelievable that you have kept the Central locally controlled and all your directors from Georgia."

"I've had to fight every step of the way to keep it well managed and prosperous enough to pay dividends—Ahhh, dessert."

The lights dimmed and the waiters marched around the table with the dessert flaming.

The instant the meal was over, Robert was

pulling back Mignonne's chair.

Eagerly, he asked, "Since you're interested in literature, perhaps you enjoy the other arts? There's a gala tonight at the Union. A concert in the opera house. Then a grand hop in the ballroom. I'd be honored to be your escort. That is if you don't mind getting out in the wet again."

"I won't melt. That sounds delightful, Mr. Edgefield." She liked the feel of his name on her tongue. "I must ask Miss Sarah Lois, but since your father is an old friend, I'm sure she will approve."

Francis Edgefield's balding head had taken on a waxen pallor. Robert eyed him dutifully.

"I should take Pa up to bed. Would it be too much to ask—would you wait?"

Her sweet face lit with a reassuring smile. "I'll need to get my cloak. I'll be glad to wait."

All the carriages were gone by the time Robert finally came down. When at last they secured one and reached the opera house, the soaring notes of violins were floating out, enticing them as they walked up the path. Colored lanterns lighted the way through the dark garden. The rain had stopped, but the evergreens glistened wetly, smelling fresh, alive.

"It seems I'm doomed to be late with you, Miss Wingate," Robert said, laughing. He joked about his difficulties in gaining an introduction.

"I wasted precious time." He shook his curly head ruefully. "Of course, I can't blame the fellows. I don't want to share you either. But I don't know why I didn't take my troubles to Pa sooner. He arranged the dinner with Colonel Wadley. From that first morning we saw you, you captured his heart—too."

He stopped beneath a bright, calcium light. With a gentle hand on each shoulder he held her so that he could look full into her face.

"That wonderful smile you gave him was the best medicine he's had in years. Far sweeter than the mineral springs."

She looked up at him wonderingly. His nose, his high cheek bones stood out with strength. The deep tones of his voice seemed so steady. She had bantered back with the flirtatious small talk of the many who had vied to dance with her. Now her throat was so filled with emotion that she could not speak. She tried to search his eyes. Deep set, they were hooded in the shadows.

A branch shook, sending a shower of sparkling drops on her green velvet gown, breaking the spell.

Laughing uncertainly, they remembered the concert.

Slipping inside, they found seats near the back where they could sit close together in the warm darkness.

She could feel the tension in his body when he leaned near. His breath was so warm and sweet upon her neck that she kept her fingers there, stroking the emeralds.

Music crashed, soared, crescendoed. Pouring

from the stage, Italian operatic selections lifted Mignonne's spirits higher, higher. Thrilled, the audience responded with such applause after each artist sang that nearly every piece was encored at least once.

When the house lights went up, they discovered that the encores had carried the concert to midnight. There could be no dance. It was Sunday morning.

Mignonne could read the disappointment in Robert's face. Since that moment in the wet garden, she had known he had been counting on the hop. Dancing was the only time a gentleman was supposed to take a lady in his arms.

She smiled at him consolingly, but she was glad the evening was ending. She was not ready to be in Robert's arms. Her emotions were lifted so high by the concert that she was afraid she would fall in love. She liked Robert more than anyone she had ever met. She wanted to stay friends.

She did not want to be hurt again.

She kept the conversation light while they returned to the Congress. But when she whirled into the bedroom she shared with Endine, she closed the door and leaned dreamily against it. The sound of the violins was still soaring within her. The music would sing in her dreams.

Brown eyes sparkling, cheeks glowing, she sighed blissfully.

Endine threw back the blanket and sat up.

"So! You're in love!"

"No! It's the concert. We're just friends."

"Friends, my Great Aunt Sophie! You're making a fool of yourself—again. I told you to set your cap for one of these Yankee millionaires. Not some penniless southerner. I told you to watch out for fortune hunters."

"But—"

"Don't say I didn't warn you. The Edgefields—senior and junior—couldn't keep their eyes off your emeralds!"

nine

Mignonne paled. "You're wrong, Endine," she said earnestly. "Those emeralds would mean nothing to them. I know about South Carolina low country because Grandma had family connections with the South Carolina Bethunes. Huge plantations were built there in the 1700s by British aristocrats. They raised rice and indigo and cotton and earned fabulous fortunes.

"Didn't you hear Colonel Wadley telling Mr. Edgefield all about my family before I was even allowed to speak to his son? Eying my emeralds indeed! I'm probably not good enough for the Edgefields."

"Maybe once they were rich, but you forget," Endine replied. "Old General Sherman only rested and gathered steam in Savannah. Burning and looting Georgia whetted the Yankee soldiers' appetites. They left South Carolina plantations more devastated than—than your folks' steamboat line."

"Oh, you always know everything!"

"Yep! Make it my business to know all." She flopped on her stomach and pulled the blankets over her frizzy head.

Mignonne threw a pillow at her. She had spoiled the lovely music.

Angrily she took off the emeralds and placed them in the jewel case. Endine was wrong. She must be! But she would wear no more borrowed jewels.

She hung the velvet dress in the armoire.

What did Endine's words matter? She and Robert Edgefield were just two friends who had shared music. . . .*Shared warm darkness. Shared cold, crisp wet-evergreen air.*

Emerald green!

Mignonne turned down the bed and jumped between clammy sheets. Wriggling irritably, she could not be still. It was as if Endine's cruel words had sprinkled the sheets with sand.

Just before dawn, she brushed away the doubts. Recapturing the lilting melodies, she relived every lovely moment of the concert and the joy of sharing it with Robert. Then she slept.

Clouds still hung low when Mignonne awakened. She hated to get up, but she was accustomed to attending church. She felt out of sorts from lack of sleep, angry with Endine for shattering the fragile beginning of her friendship with Robert. Even though she couldn't believe it, she was hurt by Endine's accusation that Robert was a fortune hunter.

The infuriating girl was unusually chipper. Endine was singing gaily, if off-key. Taking her own sweet time, she dressed in her most elaborate Sunday clothes.

Rain was falling, but only hard enough to deter the

old and infirm. Mignonne searched the crowd entering the church. Evidently, the weather had kept in Francis Edgefield. Mignonne did not give up hopes of Robert's coming until the services were well begun.

If Robert Edgefield is as dutiful a Christian as he makes himself out to be, why isn't he in church? she wondered fretfully.

Doubts washed over in a flood that made her sink down in the pew. She found no joy in the minister's words. They were merely platitudes she had heard all her life.

Her eyes roamed the congregation. It seemed hopeless to discern if anyone here was what he seemed. Was Endine's count really royalty? Was he even Spanish?

Was God of the Bible still relevant in these immoral modern times? She had learned too much from Endine about these people who sat around them singing hymns.

She recognized several American capitalists who had amassed fortunes by exploiting the country's natural resources of oil, coal, iron, and silver. While they feasted on the finest delicacies, they didn't care a fig if the poor wage-slaves who did the labor starved.

That man in the front had bought votes of whole state legislatures and bribed judges.

She noticed a man on the third row. His fingertips were together beneath his pointed black beard in a pious attitude of prayer. They called Jay Gould

the Mephistopheles of Wall Street. It was said that
the whisper of his name meant his opponents' ruin.
Even wily Commodore Vanderbilt had been out-
done and had lost the Erie Railroad to Gould's stock
market trickery.

She knew what Endine had told her was fact. This
handful of men controlled the whole country by
the power of their railroads.

The most sickening thing about the corruption
was that good people winked at it. They said nothing could be done to stop it. They merely coined a
new word for these men, robber barons.

What is God's responsibility in all this? Mignonne
wondered.

Her stomach churned, and she twisted her pearls,
her own pearls. She would no longer give the appearance of something she was not.

The organ was playing a postlude. People were
getting up. The service had ended and Mignonne
had found no answers. The world seemed such a
terrible place. She sighed. Could she even believe
there was any power left in Christianity?

That afternoon the Congress parlor was filled with
young people. Voices rose higher and higher above
the drumming of the rain. A few sleepy chaperones sat nodding in corners, wishing they could
join their elders in Sunday naps. There would be
no afternoon carriage parade today, no peace on
the piazza.

When the girls entered, Endine joined a group

crowding around the blond. She had commanded attention by bringing her parrot. He sat on her arm rolling his eyes at her as she prompted him to talk.

"What's his handicap? Give him his head!" he squawked.

Everyone laughed. The men vied to get closer to the blond on the pretext of teaching the parrot a new phrase.

Mignonne turned away. She had brought her book tucked under her arm, and she sought a settee in a corner near a gas light. She hated the dingy yellow stuff. What she wouldn't give for a cheerful kerosene lamp so she could read faster! Tom and Huck were in the cave about to find treasure.

She held the book in front of her face. She did not want Mr. Smith to see her. She was tired of his attempts at composing a poem to tell her how beautiful she was. She had heard that too much all her life. She struggled not to be vain or spoiled. She wanted to be worth something deeper.

"May I sit down?"

The timbre of the voice made her swallow. She did not have to lower the book to know it was Robert. She had tried to tell herself that she did not care if he came down. She pressed the book against her nose and lifted her almond eyes. They looked very large and white with two brown spots peeping up through the lashes searching his face.

"The boys found twelve thousand dollars," she told him solemnly. "Huck said, 'It ain't for me; I ain't used to it. . . . Looky here, Tom, being rich ain't what it's cracked up to be. It's just worry and worry, sweat and sweat, and a-wishing you was dead all the time.'"

Robert laughed quietly. "Who knows? He might be right."

Does he understand the meaning I want the quotation to convey? she wondered. His open face looked honest.

She made room for him on the small bench. He had to sit close beside her. The warmth he exuded seemed so caring.

Oh, let it be true!

With his big, sun-freckled hand supporting one side of the book, they read, held close by the pages. They had only an hour before he had to return to his father, who was in pain because of the weather. For that little time they were lost in a world of their own, oblivious to the noisy group surrounding the brassy blond.

The sun came out on Monday morning. Mignonne bounced out of bed and hurried into her clothes. Everyone would be making the most of the chance to "take the waters."

Robert always took Mr. Edgefield early and left before the fashionable crowd gathered.

Hurriedly snatching bites of a roll while she brushed her hair, Mignonne pinned on her rosebud hat, scooped up her parasol, and whirled out the door.

Dashing along the corridor with her body bent

forward, she suddenly stopped short, giggled. She seemed to hear Lily's lilting voice.

"A lady never lets anyone see her rushing."

Mignonne corrected her posture and stepped into the elevator appearing calm, serene. When she reached the street, she found that the promenade to the spring had already begun.

Shining carriages with high-stepping horses jingled along displaying drivers in livery and people dressed in their finest.

Robert was wheeling his father slowly. She quickened her step, an eager smile and greeting already on her lips.

The blond, who was seated on a shrub-encircled bench, jumped up as the men passed and asked to join them.

Mignonne hid behind the shrubbery, wondering forlornly, *Why do fairy-tale princesses always have hair of spun gold?*

Rapunzel-hair was cooing in an exaggerated drawl, the kind that gives southern belles the name of flirt.

"Ohhhh, Mr. Edgefield, Mr. Edgefield, you do say the cleverest things."

As she talked, she waved her little white hand, flashing rings on every finger. The hand hung forward, limp, signifying that it had nothing to do, would never be sullied by work. She pretended to stumble over a brick, and the hand snuck into the crook of Robert's elbow.

Mignonne watched in agony as the hussy pressed

her voluptuous body against Robert.

Now she could not go to the spring. She had nothing to do. She was all alone. Endine was attending a formal breakfast with her count. With a snort of contempt, Mignonne flopped on the bench vacated by the beautiful blond. *How could Robert be taken in by her falseness?* she wondered, scowling.

"Good morning, Mignonne. Come. Go to the spring with us," said Colonel Wadley heartily.

She could think of no excuse. She must follow him and Miss Rebecca obediently. But she hid behind them when they reached the park.

The brazen hussy had seated herself on an isolated bench so that a circle of admirers could surround her. Robert was bowing, handing her a cup of water. But she was not looking at him. She was leaning forward, elbow on knee, chin in hand, batting her eyelashes at Warren Smith. Her simpering smile tried to convey that the tale he was telling was the most fascinating thing she had ever heard. And she was wearing a parure of diamonds.

Who ever heard of putting on a whole matched set in the morning?

Through her misery, Mignonne felt Francis Edgefield's eyes smiling upon her. Hurt as she was with Robert, she must speak to the nice old gentleman.

She walked over to his wheelchair and dropped a slight curtsy. Smiling at him in spite of the angry tears in her eyes, she said, "I do hope this sunshine is making you feel better, sir."

"Good morning, Miss Wingate. Yes, much better today. Thank you for your concern. But your delightful company is a surer tonic than the waters."

"My grandma always suffered on rainy days, but when the sun came out, she was a wonder."

Forgetting herself, she turned up the cup Colonel Wadley had given her. She drank it in a gulp. A shudder shook her.

Francis Edgefield laughed heartily. "Some of the other springs taste better, don't you think?"

"I haven't been to the other springs. Colonel Wadley swears by this one. He keeps bottled Congress water all the time."

"So! You're beating my time, Pa." Robert's deep voice came from behind her. "It's a good thing Cooper isn't here. He'd steal her away entirely."

Mignonne could feel the hair on the back of her neck prickle. She did not turn to look at Robert, but she swallowed an angry retort about his being stolen by the blond. Taking a deep breath, she counted to ten, congratulating herself on wisdom and self-control.

"Robert, this little lady hasn't seen the other springs," Mr Edgefield said through slipping teeth. "Don't you think it would be the gentlemanly thing to show her the area?"

"Yes, of course, sir." Robert clicked his heels and bowed before her, but he still addressed his father. "Are you certain you feel well enough to manage all day?"

Receiving his nod, Robert looked into

Mignonne's piquant face beseechingly. "I'll hire a carriage and take you to see the geyser spring, if you'll do me the honor?"

"I. . .Oh, I'd love to," she replied, forgetting to be coy, forgetting everything but the joy of breathing when Robert was near. Then her mind filled with problems.

"Ohh! I guess I can't. Endine is going to some fancy breakfast, and, and. . .I don't have a maid to chaperone."

"We just happen to have two invitations to that fancy breakfast," Robert said with a chuckle. "We hadn't planned to use them. But if you'd like to go . . .? Perhaps if we begin there, we could work something out with Endine."

"Oh, yes. Yes. Actually, I'm famished." Her eyes were wide and sparkling. "But maybe I need to change to something more formal?"

"No. You're lovely in this white dress. I'd like for you to wear it." His cheeks reddened, but he continued, "I'll never forget that you were wearing it the first time I saw you."

Doubts and caution slipped from her shoulders. She smiled up at him in delight.

When they walked into the elegant Windsor Hotel, Mignonne was surprised to see Sarah Lois Wadley looking grand in a Gainsborough hat with a tremendous plume. It astonished her that the old maid was the personal guest of Señor DeCastro, the man who was giving the noon breakfast in honor of the

Spanish minister and his wife.

Endine bounced over to greet them. Since Mignonne had her own handsome escort, she felt safe in introducing Don Carlos Louis Pietro Valmaseda y de Castro. The tall young Spaniard, along with a *distingué* air, wore a black frock coat, light pantaloons, and white necktie. His mass of black hair was brushed upright à la Pompadour.

Mignonne grinned impishly as he kissed her hand. She tried not to laugh at his elaborate bow. She was not as well-dressed as these people, but Robert had called her lovely. She felt at home with the raven-haired Spaniards. In fact, she felt triumphant. There was not one blond head in the entire room.

Mignonne could not understand a word of the speeches, but she indulged her appetite with the most deliciously prepared food she had ever tasted.

After the breakfast, they consulted Sarah Lois.

"Yes," she agreed. "It is *en regle* to ride to the lake, but you must be properly chaperoned. I'll be delighted to go."

Senor DeCastro quickly offered his services as her escort. Arrangements were made, and the six of them were soon squeezed into a landau with the top folded back so that they would miss none of the spectacular mountain scenery.

Leaving the main thoroughfare of Saratoga, they traveled a narrow road that wound through sweet-smelling forest. Trees, leaning their arms toward one another, formed a canopy over the road, enclosing the carriage in a romantic arch.

Mignonne could feel excitement surging in Robert, an excitement that matched her own. She reminded herself that she just wanted to have fun with a friend. She did not want to fall in love. She did not want to be betrayed.

She remembered Endine's warning that the Edgefields were only interested in her jewels. Her brain, flitting over the intruding thought like a butterfly seeking brighter fare, found nectar in Robert's jokes. She settled back in the seat to enjoy the wonderful day.

She expected another spring like the Congress, boxed in with planking. Congress Spring had tiers of benches where crowds waited to be handed tin cups full of the horrid tasting stuff. But the geyser spring was a marvel such as she had never seen.

They emerged through thick woodland to see it shooting up into the air. Like a natural fountain, the water fell in sparkling clear drops that captured small rainbows. Most of the visitors were young couples seeking summer romance. They were given crystal-clear goblets to thrust into the shower. Mignonne laughed when the spray sprinkled her as she tried to catch the bubbling cascade.

Robert smiled at her over his goblet, urging her to drink.

Her dark, doe eyes looked up at him, questioning. Trusting, she received his encouraging nod and drank.

Cool, refreshing, this water seemed the thing she had been thirsting for. Was it really sweet or was it because of Robert's hand brushing hers?

Back in the carriage, they rode along, singing a sentimental old song, "Lorena":

> *The years creep slowly by, Lorena;*
>   *The snow is on the grass again;*
> *The sun's low down the sky, Lorena;*
>   *The frost gleams where the flowers*
>   *have been.*
> *But the heart throbs on as warmly now*
>   *As when the summer days were*
> *nigh.*
> *Oh, the sun can never dip so low*
>   *As down affection's cloudless sky,*
>
> *It matters little now, Lorena,*
>   *The past is the eternal past;*
> *Our hearts will soon lie low, Lorena,*
>   *Life's tide is ebbing out so fast.*
> *There is a future, o thank God!*
>   *Of life this is so small a part—*
> *'Tis dust to dust beneath the sod,*
>   *But there, up there, 'tis heart to*
> *heart.*

The Spanish gentlemen clapped appreciatively.

Then, even though they had declared after the multi-coursed breakfast that they could never eat again, they whetted growing appetites by guessing at the contents of the picnic hamper Robert had had the hotel provide.

The road dipped. A fan of branches concealed the view. Breaking through, they emerged before a shining lake. Clear blue water reflected encircling mountains and cloudless sky.

"Ohhh!" Mignonne breathed a sigh. "It looks as perfect as the mirror lake that Papa always put into the Christmas garden beneath our tree."

Spreading a blanket on the grassy bank, they unpacked the picnic with cries of delight as each item was taken from the hamper. They ate long and slowly.

Sarah Lois and Senor DeCastro became engrossed in each other's company. Her intelligent brown eyes were snapping with the pleasure of finding a stimulating conversationalist. They talked, now in Spanish, now in French, as they discussed her Grand Tour of Europe when she was young.

The two younger couples were free to stroll. Pine-covered paths beckoned them along the edge of the lake. Endine and Pietro moved on ahead.

Mignonne stopped, stretched, and looked around her. "Everything is so green and beautiful," she said.

Robert gently took her hand. With an engaging grin, he looked down at her. "Like you in your green velvet and emeralds."

She snatched her hand away, and her voice was sharp-edged as she snapped, "Mama's emeralds. Keepsakes she struggled to hold onto during the hungry days of Reconstruction."

If Robert was surprised, his thick brows hooded his eyes, and he did not show it. His voice remained even, warm. "As long as we hold onto some graciousness of living in spite of all our losses, no enemy will defeat us. Wasn't Eufaula invaded? How did your mother hide her jewels?"

"Yes, we had some terrifying moments, but we escaped by the skin of our teeth," Mignonne replied. "The invaders were sweeping upon us from the west. Having burned their way across Alabama, Grierson's troops were out of touch with the federal army. We knew that the war was over, but they did not."

Robert was listening with interest, so she continued

"It took a lot of diplomacy to hold back their torches. My Aunt Emma and some of the other ladies cooked their best meal. They served the officers with their finest silver and china and wore their silks and jewels. By treating them like gentlemen, the ladies delayed them until they received new orders not to burn and loot and steal.

"It would have been a shame to have burned Eufaula. Planters built their homes there during the period of highest prosperity when steamboats carried cotton downriver and brought back Italian marble and French antiques."

She looked at Robert closely. His blue eyes were clear as he nodded understanding. The breeze had tousled his short, sandy hair, and curls fell over his forehead.

"Eufaula is so run down now that I thought of it as old," she continued. "That is, before I saw

Savannah."

"I wish you could see Beaufort," he said eagerly. "It's even older than Savannah. It was founded by the British in 1711. We rhyme the 'Beau' with 'new,' not 'o' as you French do."

Mignonne blinked and stiffened again. Robert had certainly discovered a lot about her. Of course, there was the matter of her French-sounding name, but she had been careful not to mention her French heritage to anyone here. She thought the visitors to Saratoga were far too impressed with foreigners. They fawned over royalty.

"I'm really not that French, you know." She laughed falsely, but she tried to explain. "My great-grandmother was French. Her people were Bonapartists exiled because of their claim to the throne of France. They settled around the river port of Demopolis, Alabama. The refugees tried to grow olives and grapes, but they failed and turned to cotton. Papa's people had a steamboat line, but most of the steamers were sacrificed in the war. Papa and Foy, Mama's brother, have been struggling to get started again."

Robert's candid face told her that he took each person at his or her own.

"It's obvious that you have a very warm and close family," he said. "I envy you that."

They strolled down the shore to a rustic bench. He brushed it off, urging her to sit so that he could tell her about his home.

"Combahee is quite a ways out from Beaufort.

Our plantation is named for the river. The house is built on raised foundations of tabby. Wide, two-story porches face the river. You can sit on either story with a glass of iced tea in hand and catch the salty breeze. You see, the river is really tidewater lapping the low country islands. It's relaxing and peaceful to look out across the blue water and green marshes."

Mignonne clasped her hands in delight. Eyes sparkling, she exclaimed, "It sounds wonderful! I'm so glad your home escaped, too."

"Yes." Robert's smooth jaw worked with tension. "But only because it was being used as a hospital and was filled with Confederate wounded."

She waited, sensing he needed to say more.

"Because they couldn't burn the house, they were bound, bent, and determined to destroy everything else on the plantation. I was just a kid, but I can see them now, burning every barn and fence and rice mill and. . . ." His voice trailed away.

Then from deep inside he brought up agonized words. "Mother couldn't stand the shock. It killed her as surely as if they'd shot her. She'd just borne twins, and she lay there three months unable to get up. . . .And died."

"I'm so sorry!" she gasped. Reaching out, she brushed her fingers over his big, sun-browned hand. Hurting for the little boy who had grown up yearning for his mother, she longed to hold his hand, but he did not try to take hers again. She sorely regretted that Endine's wisp of doubt had made her snatch it away.

Robert smiled at her wistfully. Suddenly brisk, he said, "Our dream is to restore Combahee to her former beauty. We—my father and my older brother and I—have diversified. Growing rice took more labor than we can afford. Now we're trying everything we can think of. We're even trying to raise Arabian horses."

He stretched widely. She thought he was going to put his arm across the bench around her. He didn't.

"The soil is still there, the water, the trees. The evenness of the salt marshes speaks to me of the vastness of God's love. And—I've noticed how much you like trees. . . ."

"Yes."

"God's infinite caring is shown in the different forms of trees. I'd like for you to see our unique live oaks. They're like ancient ladies protecting everything, gracious all the while in their shawls of Spanish moss."

Mignonne wondered why she had thought of Robert Edgefield as quiet. His eloquence had touched her heart, her mind, her soul.

Sunset was turning the scene into an impressionistic painting. The lake was alight with streaks of pink and gold. Mignonne wished that she could capture it on canvas as Adrianna would have done. She wanted to remember every detail. She recalled her mother observing that she was rushing through life. Why had she suddenly changed? She felt so content. She did not care what might be happening elsewhere. She wanted nothing but to sit by Robert.

But Miss Sarah Lois was beckoning. Mignonne feared their idyll must end.

Reluctantly they walked back. They discovered that Miss Sarah Lois was grinning like a schoolgirl.

"Come. Let's move on," she said. "The restaurant around the shore provides rowboats."

ten

"Don't miss the sunset," Robert said to the chattering group packing up the picnic hamper.

They turned and fell silent as they watched.

Waiting for a moment suspended in time, the sun slipped behind the far off mountain, leaving only her cloak of golden mist. Coolness, tranquility drifted from the lake, placid now except for tiny ripples reaching for the last sunbeams.

With sighs of contentment, they climbed into the carriage and rode along quietly through shadowy forest. The soft sounds of twilight and pairing birds soothed each one to savoring a perfect day.

By the time they reached the far side of the lake, darkness had fallen. At first it looked as if the stars had followed a pathway down the mountainside into the lake. They realized the twinkling lights on the shore were torches when they heard snatches of music and laughter. The tantalizing aroma of frying fish and bubbling stews drifted out from the restaurant. Laughing at their own shamelessness, they decided to eat again and save the boat ride for last.

They ordered everything on the menu: black bass, brook trout, woodcock, reed birds, canvasbacks, and soft shell crabs. They had great fun sharing tastes from each other's selection of food, all of which was exotic to Mignonne. There was a great stir when the waiter brought out the specialty of the restaurant, something called Saratoga chips. Amazed, they nibbled at the potatoes cut thin as tissue paper and crackly like popcorn.

As they ate, it seemed they had all become old friends. Laughter rang to the overhanging rafters in the rustic restaurant. Robert regaled them with stories of three men trying to cope with twin girls who delighted in switching identities to fool them.

At last they sat back, satiated.

"Part of the fun of traveling is trying the native dishes," Mignonne declared. "I believe this freshly caught black bass is the most delicious food I have ever eaten."

Freckles shined on Robert's face as he grinned like an eager little boy. "I'm so glad you enjoy sea-food. I know you'll love our low country cookouts with shrimp and rice and cornbread and she-crab soup."

Mignonne glanced up sideways through the corner of her lashes. She was afraid to look directly at him because her heart beat suddenly faster at the hint in his words. She must be careful. This dark lake ringed with mysterious mountains was the most romantic place she had ever been. She must not let herself be carried away by dreams.

After the meal, they walked out onto the dock. A full moon had risen, illuminating the water. Joking that a boat would sink under the weight of all they had eaten, they rented one anyway. The two chaperones sat in the stern. Sarah Lois placed her parasol between them for propriety's sake.

Robert stepped into the bow and helped Mignonne with a protective arm around her waist. They remained close, drawing warmth needed in the crisp mountain air.

Pietro and Endine took the center. The elegant young count had brought a fine guitar. Striking intense chords, he thrilled them with swift fingers flying over classical Spanish music. Then he strummed softly in slow sweet rhythms of romance while the boat floated on the path of moonbeams.

The morning sun kissed a smile on Mignonne's lips. She bounded out of bed eager to begin a new day.

Endine clattered down the stairs, leaving her, but she wanted to ride in the elevator.

She sat on the damask-cushioned bench feeling as if the slowly descending wire cage were Cinderella's coach. Below stood Robert, watching for her, waiting.

He was hiding something behind his back.

When she alighted, he bowed low and presented her a nosegay encircled in a lace doily. From a circle of smooth green leaves rose spikes with inconspicuous white blossoms.

"Mignonette!" she exclaimed. She accepted the shaggy white flowers and sniffed their delicate fragrance. She knew Endine would tell her mignonette might be a garden favorite in America, but in

Europe it was considered a weed. She would never listen to Endine again. She was enchanted by the thoughtfulness behind his gift.

"However did you find something so. . .special?"

Robert's cheekbones reddened. He was bursting with pleasure that she knew the significance of his gift.

"I found a florist with the soul of a poet. He understood that I must have the perfect flower for the perfect girl. I didn't need him to tell me that mignonette means 'dainty darling.'"

Blissfully, they wandered outside. An omnibus was loading with young couples. With a quick nod of agreement, they jumped aboard, neither knowing nor caring where it was going.

The large public vehicle followed a different road from the one they had taken the previous day. This one wound through sunlit, cultivated fields. Neat farm houses were set amid gardens and orchards burgeoning with reds and golds, foretelling the promise of autumn.

The lumbering omnibus stopped. The happy group walked along a path through dark forest. There were squeals from some of the girls when they had to cross a swinging bridge. Mignonne had to close her eyes and hold onto the rope webbing on each side. In the middle the whole bridge was swaying back and forth, creaking. She stopped. Robert's arm was protectively near. She looked down at the stream tumbling in milky foam over a rocky bed.

At the end of the path was Excelsior Spring. They quenched their thirst with the sweetest water of all.

That afternoon, when the parade of carriages began along Broadway, they walked.

The stores were filled with the latest New York fashions, but the tables set up along the street drew their attention. There were vendors of all kinds.

Promenading Saratoga's Broadway was like attending a great, fancy fair. Mignonne and Robert stopped to watch a sidewalk show. A girl in fringed buckskins was singing comical songs. When a crowd had gathered and was relaxed, laughing, a fast-talking man stepped up to sell quack medicine.

Endine lingered beside displays of antiques. She hovered over a tray of Oriental jewelry, fingering each piece longingly until Pietro bought her a bracelet.

Mignonne had never seen Indians. Their silent dignity touched her tender heart. She browsed the tables of their wares and smiled tentatively, but she received no answering smile. She shook her head when Robert asked her to select something. He insisted and bought a small piece of Indian jewelry.

That evening when she dressed for the hop, she placed the trinket on a velvet ribbon and tied it about her slender neck for a charming choker.

The hotel garden was crowded with gentlemen who clamored to fill her dance card. She felt obliged to let them, but she secretly saved all of her waltzes for Robert Edgefield.

As she danced the German with Mr. Smith, she

wondered if it gave Robert the stab of pain she felt when he whirled by in the arms of the blond from Baltimore.

The next morning, Endine was up early. Her mouth was pursed, and her eyes rolled nervously as she hurried through her toilette. She went out the door with only a crisp, "See ya."

Did she have a secret assignation with Pietro? But, no, she had dressed carelessly.

Mignonne rolled over on her back and stretched luxuriously. It was marvelous to be alone. She had no need to hurry. She could preen and sigh and let herself enjoy being a little bit in love with Robert. These last few days had been the kind of summer romance to remember for the rest of her life.

It was obvious that Robert wanted to spend his time with her, and last night before they parted he had secured her promise to attend the croquet tournament with him.

They were to meet at ten o'clock. She had time to dress slowly, carefully.

She sprinkled lilac bath salts into the walnut-boxed tub and lay back, singing snatches of "Lorena" while the perfume drifted up around her.

The fragrance made her decide to wear a dress she had been pushing back in the armoire as too old for her. The bodice was soft lilac crepe with a deep ruffle around the V-neck and sleeves that daringly showed a bit of her forearms. The bustled skirt was deep purple taffeta that rustled delightfully when she walked.

Surveying herself in the looking glass, she decided that when she married—if she ever married—her bridesmaids' dresses would be this color.

"And hats just like this," she said aloud as she tilted the point over one eye. Talented Adrianna had simply cut a heart out of cardboard, covered it with taffeta, and added a nosegay of lavender and purple tulips. Instead of gloves, she pulled on fingerless lace mitts.

She consulted the watch pinned over her heart. There was time to make a leisurely approach to the croquet court on the lawn where Robert would be waiting.

Robert was dressed in a new claw hammer coat as blue as his eyes.

All of the players wore regulation whites. They stood out sharply against the emerald lawn. It was cut to velvet smoothness by newly invented hand lawn mowers. Some of the contestants were nervously clutching their lucky mallets. All were taking the game seriously. They lined up at the starting stake.

Mignonne chose her champion immediately, a girl who drove her wooden ball smartly through the first set of wickets.

The girl proceeded quickly through the proscribed course of arches and hit the far stake. She had started back when an opponent's ball struck hers.

The opponent placed his wooden ball against the girl's ball. Putting his foot on his ball, he struck it a sharp blow with his mallet. Her ball had been just short of the goal post. Now it was sent flying away.

Mignonne clapped her hand over her mouth to smother a shriek. "How mean! Is that fair?"

Robert laughed. "That's what it means to croquet. He has completed his circuit, but he's dallying, waiting to see what damage he can do. As long as he hasn't hit the home stake, he's free to be a rover."

"And spoil her winning. I hate that part. I've tried to play. But I never was any good. Aunt Jeanne has an antique set she calls 'pail mail.' But I couldn't master it. Watching these people play makes croquet look simple. But when I try it I just hit the side of the wicket." She nodded her head for emphasis, and tulips trembled on her heart-shaped hat.

Chuckling softly, Robert was watching her instead of the game.

I never noticed how cute he looks when his eyes crinkle up at the corners, she thought.

He bent close and whispered, "After the match if the course is free, I'll teach you how to play."

When the tournament ended and the trophies had been awarded, the crowd still lingered, but the court was empty. Mignonne and Robert selected mallets and stepped shyly onto the smooth lawn.

Mignonne tapped her ball. It went nowhere.

"See? I told you."

Robert laughed. "Don't be so impatient," he said. "It takes firmness of wrist and a true eye. Let me show you how to hold the mallet."

He bent her shoulders and showed her how to position her feet apart for the proper stance. Standing behind her, he closed his arms around her. His fingers shaped her wrists and placed her hands on the mallet.

She could feel the texture of his crisp linen coat through her soft crepe. Her ruffled sleeves fell back, baring wrists and fingers that tingled with his touch. His tanned face was close enough to inhale the warm fragrance of her porcelain skin. His breath felt sweet on the nape of her neck.

Softly, he brushed his mustache across her spine. Stiffening, they stood still holding the mallet. Then, ever so gently, he kissed the curve at the back of her neck.

Feelings she had never experienced were bubbling up like the geyser spring. Turning in his arms, she looked into his face. He was as shaken as she.

People were chattering and milling about all around them. It seemed strange, special, that although they had contrived moments in the moonlight, they had waltzed in each other's arms, they had felt only a sense of waiting. Now, amid a crowd, in broad open daylight, in a moment unplanned, unexpected, binding currents passed between them.

There was no more holding back. Whether it brought joy or pain, Mignonne knew in that moment that she was deeply in love with Robert Edgefield.

Suddenly he remembered the croquet ball and struck it with the forgotten mallet. The ball bounced off the wicket, rolled lopsidedly, and dropped off the court. It landed in the gutter. They laughed uncertainly.

Suddenly behind them a staccato noise made them blink and turn.

With high heels hitting the sidewalk, Endine was stamping along in a fury. Her hair, no longer mimosa pink, stuck out behind her like an orange flame.

Mignonne's eyes widened in astonishment. She felt near hysteria from the confusing surge of emotions, and she could not help bursting out laughing. She laughed until she wiped tears.

Robert stood behind her rubbing his mustache and trying unsuccessfully not to laugh.

"It's not funny!" Endine stormed, aiming an elbow toward Mignonne's ribs.

"I'm sorry," she said, side-stepping the blow. "But what in the world did you do?"

"I wheedled Miss McPheeter into telling me the name of the hairdresser who colors her hair. I wanted mine gold."

"What? Miss McWho?"

"McPheeter. You know. That blond hussy from Baltimore. You aren't innocent enough to think her hair *grew* that way, are you?"

She clawed at her stiff orange mane and demanded stormily, "Do you think she had her woman do this on purpose?"

"I doubt it," said Robert, no longer able to stop laughing.

"McPheeter has a horse in the race this afternoon. I hope he comes in l. . .last! Endine began to cry. "We've got to go to the races." She snuffed. "Tomorrow evening is my only chance. My last chance to be with Pietro. The Spanish minister is l. . .leaving tomorrow for Washington to visit the p. . .president. I may never see Pietro again!"

Endine exploded in a loud wail.

People were staring, and Mignonne patted and shushed.

"Endine, I'm sorry, but I don't want to go to the races because—"

"I'll take you," put in Robert, suddenly sober. "Endine needs us. And it would be a different experience for you. Everyone must go to the races at least once before they leave Saratoga."

"Leave?" Mignonne's brain could not function beyond that word.

eleven

Leave? Mignonne struggled with the forbidding thought. Her head was whirling. She steadied herself with her croquet mallet as if the ground were slipping out from under her. *We can't go! Not just as I've found how much I love Robert!*

Hadn't Colonel Wadley said they'd stay ten more days? Had she lost track? Time was strung with golden moments of seeing Robert, of hearing his voice.

His voice. What was he saying? She looked at him blankly.

"Mignonne, you can't leave without one day at the races," Robert repeated. "Saratoga's races have become a national event since the war."

She frowned.

He hurried on, persuading. "Families go. You'll feel at home. The ladies section of the grandstand is covered with church cushions."

She laughed uncertainly.

"You don't have to gamble," Endine put in scornfully.

"Gambling is a sore subject in our family," Mignonne explained. "Foy—Mama's brother— risked all we had on a steamboat race. He came within a gnat's eyebrow of losing the boat he'd

111

named for me—and everything!"

"I understand." Robert's voice was grave. "Our family has a problem gambler, too. My brother, Cooper."

They looked at each other, empathizing without words.

Seeing that they were becoming absorbed in each other again, Endine plucked at Mignonne's sleeve to get her attention.

"It's my last day to see Pietro," she wailed. "I need you! Besides, you should see a race. Everyone who is anyone in the whole country will be there." She gasped, remembering the more immediate problem of her flaming orange hair.

"Oh, nooo! Come on, Min, you've got to help me *do* something!" Tears streamed down her freckled face.

With a quick goodbye to Robert, Mignonne followed Endine to their room.

They soaped and scrubbed and poured pitcher after pitcher of water over Endine's head.

Mignonne surveyed her, hands on hips. "It's no use. Whatever the hairdresser did, it won't come out. The color only gets brassier."

Endine flung herself on the bed, sobbing. She refused to leave the bed and for the rest of the day remained with a pillow over her head.

The next morning, Mignonne sprang out of her bed shouting, "I have an idea!" She ran to her trunk and began rummaging.

"Get up, get up," she commanded the red-eyed Endine. Triumphantly, she whipped out a long strip of bright, multi-colored silk. "I've always loved to watch Kitty wrap her turbans. Sit! Sit in that chair and don't move."

Inexpertly she wound the cloth. It fell apart. She tried again, binding the silk more tightly and tucking the ends. Pulling an egret feather from another hat, she stuck it in the turban and stood back.

"Voila! A new style for Saratoga."

Endine looked in the mirror, wiped her tear-splotched face, and sniffled.

"Minnie, you're a true friend."

Convulsed by silly giggles, they hurried to dress. Mignonne chose a smart black-and-white striped chambray trimmed with black velvet bows. Her wide straw hat and parasol had matching ribbon.

They decided that to best show off the turban, Endine should wear stark white.

The races were to begin at eleven o'clock. Making sure that the turban was securely covering Endine's orange hair, they hurried down the long piazza to meet Robert and Pietro.

They were stopped. Old ladies in rocking chairs wanted to see the turban. Saratoga was always searching for something new. For once, Mignonne's beauty went unnoticed. Endine had to travel a gauntlet of outrageous compliments. The girls clutched their stomachs and shook, trying to hold back giggles.

At that moment, Miss McPheeter made a grand

entrance. Golden head erect, body bent forward, she swished down the piazza, drawing an especially long train behind her. The trailing gown was piled with twists of ruffles and a confusion of puffs. Each puff was adorned with a bow and floating streamers. She promenaded slowly for all to see. The train twitched right, then left; then it received a gentle shake.

"An old hen settling her ruffled feathers," Mignonne whispered.

"The Saratoga wriggle," Endine hissed.

Everyone stood back waiting as Miss McPheeter folded her multitude of material into the tandem brought around for her by John Henry Keen. His prancing team led the line of elegant equipages, landau with the tops thrown back to display their owners costly toilettes, barouche with drivers in gorgeous livery.

When a magnificent Brewster coach, black with yellow running gear, drawn by four prancing bays stopped at the carriage block, Pietro stepped forward and opened the door with a flourishing bow. The girls were astounded that this was what he and Robert had hired for today.

Even through her misgivings, Mignonne was caught up in the excitement as they joined the parade. Indeed, all of Saratoga was going to the races.

The racetrack, set amid the elms and pines, was abloom with flowered hats and parasols. People were strolling about to see and be seen. There were ladies here, even walking through the paddocks.

When they took their seats in the grandstand, Mignonne was pleased that there really were church cushions on them. Still, she felt out of her element, especially when she looked down and saw a motley group of women wearing layers of rouge and rice powder.

Down front in special seats sat William Vanderbilt's family. Over there was Jay Gould. These men who stole railroads and millions of dollars from one another were now in seemingly friendly competition for their favorite horses. The smell of their strong black cigars drifted up, fouling the clean, dry air.

Mignonne's narrowed eyes peered over the programme with which she covered her face. If she was surprised at the number of ladies, she was amazed that many were provided with little books and pencils. As race followed race, they kept them in constant use. Money passed through jeweled fingers.

"If a lady must wager, she should do it in private," she said primly.

Robert laughed. "Forget the betting and enjoy the beauty of the horses. Watch Harry Bassett. He's the favorite to win the Kenner stakes."

The horse he pointed out was eager to enter the race. Muscles rippling, eyes flashing, nostrils flaring, he careened madly upon the turf. Suddenly he reared, plunged.

Mignonne gasped as the jockey went flying over

his head. The small black man brushed off his colorful silks and remounted.

Harry Bassett did win, but she found the brief race less exciting than the thrill of being beside Robert. This was the first really hot day she had spent in Saratoga. The heat was making curls escape his neatly combed hair.

She imagined twirling one around her finger. Her breath came faster whenever his hand brushed hers on the seat between them. Yet, she was delighted to discover they could still be friends. She had been misled in thinking passion and friendship could not exist together. Robert never pushed her as Paul had done. With Robert she felt safe, secure, cherished.

Between races, they discussed the next night's ball.

"Why is it different from the usual hop in the garden?" Mignonne was proud she remembered not to say cotillion.

"Aw, Minnie. This is a grand, full-dress ball."

"The Congress rolls out the red carpet—literally," Robert said. "It stretches all the way across the high bridge that arches over the street connecting the ballroom of Congress Hall with the hotel."

His blue eyes crinkled and his eager face shone. "By the time you reach the end of it, you'll see why it's called the 'Bridge of Smiles.'"

"Everyone will wear their best ball gowns and jewels," Endine said. "But we need to start planning some unique costumes for the fourteenth. Oh, Pietro, can't you come back from Washington for the masquerade that ends the season?"

Pietro smoothed his black pompadour with the heel of his hand and shook his head sorrowfully. Although he usually said little, he managed to convey in his heavily accented English that he wanted to wager with Endine on the next race for one of her red curls.

Giggles escaped, but they bit their cheeks to stifle laughter.

Endine ran her fingers around her turban to make certain no orange hair had escaped. "No," she said. "Best not wager. I might offend Miss Mignonne, who considers gambling a terrible iniquity."

Pietro's reply was interrupted by the bugle.

Horses for the third race, the summer handicap, were paraded past the judges' stand, past the grandstand. Robert explained the handicap of varying weight pads that different horses carried. The favorite, a dark chestnut, was carrying one hundred fifteen pounds.

The roar of the crowd shouting for the chestnut infected Mignonne with excitement. She was laughing and clapping when he beat Miss McPheeter's horse.

Hot, thirsty, Robert and Mignonne climbed down from the grandstand to search for something cold to drink. He left her for a moment.

Standing alone by the paddock, she suddenly had a sense of eyes roaming over her. Mignonne tried to ignore a very tall man. She changed her parasol to her opposite shoulder to place a screen between them. Accustomed to being noticed pleasantly, she felt unnerved by this man's gaze. He was eyeing her far too intimately.

Where was Robert? She moved to follow him.

The hairy man stepped in front of her.

Sweeping off his hard black derby, he bowed over her hand. He had kissed it before she could snatch away.

"Such a stunning beauty as this can only be Mademoiselle Min-yonne." he said in a slow, flat drawl. "James Cooper Edgefield at your service, ma'am."

"Cooper!" Robert appeared solidly beside her. "What're you doing here?" His voice was harsh. "Among other things, you're supposed to be at home looking after the twins."

Cooper tapped the derby, sliding it low over his eyes so that his slant-eyed gaze surveyed them lazily. He shrugged. "You'll know in a few minutes anyway. I've entered Combahee in the steeplechase. What about you? You're supposed to be stayin' at the hotel nursing Pa."

"Does Pa know you're racing Combahee?"

"I can bet he will now."

"What possessed you to risk Combahee? You know we've sunk every penny we've got in him for bloodline."

"Exactly! Every penny, little brother. In case you hadn't thought of it, taxes are comin' due as sure as the leaves are fallin' off the trees."

"What about Ruth and Rubye?"

"They're safe enough with Mammy." He laughed. "Course who's t'say how safe she is with them? Those brats! I had to get away fo' awhile. They're always fighting over who'll get the pink and who'll get the blue—"

"Don't change the subject. We must strike Combahee from the race."

"'Spect it's too late now. The steeplechase is about to begin."

While they argued, Mignonne looked from one scowling face to the other. Older, a good three inches taller, Cooper had leaner cheeks and more perfect features. There was a family resemblance in the deep-set eyes and straight nose, but his hair was darker. Unruly curls showed underneath the derby. Hair grew on down beside his ears and along his jawline in muttonchop whiskers. She preferred Robert's clean-cut looks, but in all honesty, she had to admit Cooper was more handsome.

The real difference lay deeper. Robert was a man governed by duty.

Cooper doesn't hit the home stake, she thought. *He stays a rover.*

Robert had the healthy, ruddy look of someone who worked outdoors. Cooper had a cultivated tan. She'd bet if he took off his shirt, he'd be tanned. . .

Blushes reddened her hot face. Why had such a foreign thought come into her head? Cooper frightened her. She felt like the small jockey thrown by Harry Bassett. There was more virility in Cooper than she knew how to handle.

Made nervous by the hostility bristling on each side of her, Mignonne walked back to the races between the brothers.

The steeplechase was novel and exciting, especially when they pointed out their beautiful red-gold stallion, Combahee. Barriers had been set up. The horses went flying over green turf, but now they were leaping hedges and stone walls. Beyond the walls were pools of water.

Mignonne screamed when Combahee took a wall too low. At the last second, he lifted and soared over wall and water without wetting a hoof.

Several jockeys were thrown over the horses' heads in the mad gallop. They gained her admiration by courageously remounting and rushing onward to their goal.

Robert tensed as the horse ahead of Combahee fell and obviously broke his leg.

Nearing the finish, Combahee moved out.

"Give him his head!" Cooper yelled. "Let him run his own race!"

Robert's hand searched for hers. She held on, sharing his concern.

Combahee lost.

Mignonne was heedlessly jostled between two pairs of broad, stiff shoulders.

twelve

The next morning Mignonne rode down in the elevator holding her breath, wondering what the day would bring forth. Confused, ill at ease, she clasped both hands over her heart when she looked down upon a curly head and blue linen coat. She was happy to see Robert alone. With Cooper around, Robert had once again become shy.

In fact, Robert had retreated into an ominous silence after Combahee's luckless race. Robert needed encouragement. Forgetting about herself and thinking only of him, she formed a cheery greeting on smiling lips.

The man looked up. It was not Robert, after all. It was Cooper.

There was no stopping the elevator's descent. And Cooper was already bowing low, opening the iron door, helping her step from her bird cage.

"Good morning," she said politely. "Where's—"

"Little brother? Oh he's fetching and carrying. Pa's calling fo' this and fo' that to be put by his bed. Robert told me to come on and take you for a stroll around the garden. You and I need to get acquainted."

"Oh, but that's taking your time. I'll be quite all right—"

"Nonsense! I'm proud to be seen escorting the prettiest filly in Saratoga," he said, putting her hand in the crook of his elbow and giving it a pat.

She swallowed. She had ambivalent feelings about Cooper. She was pleased that Robert's brother admired her. Something about the virility he exuded made her want to preen and be her prettiest. That something made her flutter her eyelashes flirtatiously at the tall man of the world.

She regretted her action immediately. He twirled the corner of his well-waxed mustache and winked wickedly. Guiding her across the piazza, he led her into the dew-fresh garden. The beautiful park beside the hotel was already filling with people walking for their health, but he led her to a secluded path that had tall shrubs screening the view of onlookers. There were twists and nooks that afforded long moments of privacy.

Cooper was keeping up a flow of casual conversation, but he was holding her far too close against him. She pulled her hand from his arm on the pretense of fixing her parasol.

With a more breathable space between them, she asked. "What about your father? How did he take the news of Combahee's race?"

Cooper laughed. "When he has time to think about it, he'll understand. Saratoga's August horse races have been a national event since 1864. Even having a horse good enough to enter will help us to make a name for our horse farm."

"That makes sense," Mignonne replied.

"If Combahee could have won, we'd have made a killing because of the odds on what I bet. It would have been enough to pay our debts and taxes. We'd have started on the road to living in the manner to which the Edgefields have become accustomed."

She watched him as his eyes narrowed and his voice hardened. Suddenly she noticed that he had lost the flat drawl.

He only talked that way to further irritate Robert, she realized.

"Actually. . .," Cooper laughed. "We haven't gotten around to telling Pa that either the horse or the black sheep of the family is in Saratoga."

"Oh, but isn't that risky?" The deception frightened her. It offended her scruples even more than his gambling. "What if someone tells him. Or—or what if he *sees* you?"

"Yeah. Some busybody might tell him. But he won't see me. Not 'til I'm ready. Robert says he's too sick to leave his room right now. He came here under doctor's orders. They say the mineral waters of these springs are so beneficial that even in colonial days people risked wilderness travel to drink them."

"I wonder how they knew about the springs with the mountains." She gestured toward the rugged Adirondacks.

"Oh, the Indians had been using them for their good medicine. People claim all kinds of impossible curative powers, but physicians have declared them helpful for heart and artery problems and rheumatism and digestion. Robert says Pa's digestion has improved, but otherwise he's no better."

"Don't you 'spose part of the value of being here is resting and relaxing and forgetting everyday—"

She did not finish. She had caught a note of real concern in Cooper's voice, yet she wondered what would happen when Francis Edgefield learned he was here.

"Tell me about the twins," she said, changing the subject. "I know they must be cute."

"Cute? I guess. Ruth's a tomboy. Rubye shows flashes of growing into a woman. Not having a mother, they're pretty independent."

Cooper seemed to have lost interest in the conversation. He was looking over her shoulder. He urged her into a bright center garden where red geraniums, white petunias, and blue alyssum were planted in spectacular beds glowing in full sunlight.

"Would you do me the honor of letting me escort you to the ball tonight?" Cooper asked in a serious tone.

Surprised, Mignonne considered him. Was he really interested in her, or had he always snatched the toys from his little brother? She struggled to keep her voice even.

"Why, thank you, Copper. That's gallant of you, but I've already accepted Robert's invitation. Let me introduce you to someone."

She thought of Endine upstairs in their room wallowing in tears now that Pietro was gone. Endine had stormily declared she was not going to the ball with such atrocious hair. But if a man as tall and handsome as Cooper was available, she would, no doubt, change her mind.

Cooper was shaking his head.

"No. There's no one else here as beautiful as you are. If I can't be your escort, I'll just go alone. I'd better keep myself available in case Pa's sick and Robert can't go."

"So! Here you are."

The deep voice behind her made Mignonne jump.

"Well, speak o' the devil," drawled Cooper.

"I'd hoped you might wait for me in the parlor," Robert said accusingly.

The whites of her eyes shown large and surprised at the coldness of Robert's voice and the hurt on his face.

"But—but Cooper said you weren't. . . . That you told him to take me walking, and. . ." She compressed her lips.

"I didn't."

"Well, little brother, you were busy, and I'd 'a sworn that—" He shrugged. "You were late."

"And you took advantage." Robert's eyebrows bristled as he glared at Cooper.

Mignonne put up her parasol and strode away. Before she could reach the piazza, they caught up with her.

"We're sorry."

"We're sorry. Come on. Let's walk down Broadway and see what there is to see."

"Only if you behave."

"We promise." They spoke in unison with mock contrition on their faces and their hats over their hearts in pledge.

Mignonne was not accustomed to handling two men at once, but they spent a pleasant morning looking in the shops along Broadway. Vying to please her, they turned into the most jovial escorts.

At noon, she dined with them at the Edgefield table in the Congress Hall dining room. By the custom of Saratoga, this was the largest of the many meals of the day. Usually she enjoyed the courses of rich food, but today she was not hungry.

The two men proposed various pursuits for the afternoon, but she firmly declined.

"Let us take you to White Sulphur Spring," said Cooper. "It's different. The water has a yellow tint. There's no telling what it might cure us of." He laughed good-naturedly.

"No. I have a new book, and I shall spend the afternoon resting and reading."

"Then meet us for supper at six-thirty," said Robert.

She shook her head. "I'll see you at eight-thirty for the ball."

She escaped them quickly. She really wanted to wash her hair and wrap it in curl papers. Somehow, even though there had been hops in the garden most of the evenings since they had been in Saratoga, she sensed this ball was going to be different. She was nervous.

As supper time approached, the sounds in the

hotel corridor told her she was not the only one not going down to supper. She could hear the hurried steps of waiters and the clinking of glass on supper trays. When she stuck her curlered head out the door to take their tray, she could hear squeals and splashings of water from adjoining rooms. Excitement was in the air. There was a constant ringing of bells. Chambermaids and bellboys scurried with various errands.

Darkness came early because of low hanging clouds. It already seemed like night, and Mignonne began trying to coax her hair into curls for a formal style. She was peering into the looking glass when suddenly the gaslights sputtered. They went out.

Shrieks could be heard all up and down the hall as ladies were left in the dark.

"Don't worry," Endine said from beneath her pillow. "Happens all the time. Just wait for the Saratoga dip."

After minutes that seemed interminable, there was a tap at the door. Mignonne opened it a crack and was faced with the whites of eyes over flickering flame. The corridor was a ghostly scene as servants moved slowly, passing out dipped tallow candles.

Mignonne completed dressing by the dim light. She laughed nervously. "I'll look all right if the ball is held by candlelight."

In spite of the problems, she was ready too soon. Feeling a tightness in her chest, she sat down. Fiddling with strands of hair that threatened to slip down the back of her neck, she waited apprehensively for the clock to strike eight-thirty.

Just as the chimes began, they were accompanied by a tooting and squeaking. The orchestra was tuning up. Then there was a drumming on the window. Rain.

thirteen

At the moment Mignonne entered the parlor, it burst into dazzling light. The lamplighter stood at work beneath the magnificent crystal chandelier, which was used only on grand occasions.

Caught in the spotlight, she hoped her appearance was adequate. She had chosen her favorite dress, the pink silk organza she had worn for Libba's wedding. She had only to see the joy in Robert's eyes and the shine on his cheeks to know that everything was fine.

"You're lovely as a rose," he whispered. Bowing, he shyly presented her with a dainty spray of pink rosebuds.

"You always know the perfect thing," she said with delight.

She had swept her shining black hair on top of her head, and now she stood before the pier mirror in the parlor and pinned the rosebuds on one side of the mass of curls bobbing over her forehead. Framed by the roses and the sheer pink ruffle caressing her chin, her pixie face was enchanting.

Suddenly her reflection included two men. The brothers looked even taller in long tailcoats, even handsomer in elegant brocade waistcoats and white ties. Cooper had been true to his word, for once. It was apparent that he was joining them. She took a steadying breath before she turned to face him.

Cooper bowed, all gentlemanly politeness. He handed her a large corsage tied with yellow ribbon.

"Thank you," she said, tying the flowers over the wrist of her elbow-length white kid gloves.

She rewarded him with a smile. She was pleased that Robert's brother liked her, but she was also disappointed. She had dreamed that tonight would be a special time of dancing in Robert's arms.

"Are you ready to travel the 'Bridge of Smiles'?" asked Robert.

Afraid to trust her voice, she nodded. She took the arm Robert offered with her left hand and Cooper's with her right.

They stepped onto the red carpet which had been rolled out to the parlor and followed it to the side door.

The red carpet continued up the bridge fifty feet above the noisy traffic of horses and carriages on the street below, onto a level with the treetops. Rain pattered on the blue-and-white striped awning covering the bridge. It awakened the evergreens, and their spicy fragrance seemed to add even more excitement to the crisp night air.

The carpeted way spanned the entire distance from the hotel to the ballroom suspended halfway up the hillside. With myriads of lights, the ballroom beckoned them, sparkling as if the stars had gathered on the mountain to dance.

Mignonne had never felt so magically happy.

Music drifted down, surrounding them with symphonic sound. Not the mere band from the hop, this was a full orchestra with a multitude of throbbing violins.

Robert and Cooper had reconciled their differences—at least temporarily—and with teasing, jousting rivalry, they vied to please her.

With feet skimming the carpet, she walked across the bridge between the brothers.

When the handsome trio entered the ballroom, all eyes turned upon them. In her simple gown ornamented with a single tulle blossom at her tiny waistline, Mignonne looked like a fresh rose.

Mirrored walls reflected the lights from tremendous multi-branched brass chandeliers. Fire was caught in the flashing facets of the ladies' jewels. Their scoop-necked gowns of silks and satins were trimmed with ribbons and feathers and long, elaborate trains.

Mignonne untied her wrap. The little cape, which had made her gown demure for an afternoon wedding, slipped away. The wide, portrait neckline of the dress beneath the ruffled chiffon cape had only the merest hint of sleeve. Her creamy shoulders and her swan-like neck were revealed. On her porcelain skin was a glowing necklace of astonishing pink rubies.

Cooper's eyebrows shot up and his waxed mustache drooped over his gaping mouth. Then his eyes narrowed, gleaming avariciously.

Tensing, Mignonne saw what she had been trying to deny. Cooper's intentions fairly bristled.

Wary fingers flew to her throat. She wet her lips and spoke with her words tumbling over one another.

"Aren't Aunt Emma's rubies exquisite? One can see why Uncle Jonathan dared to run the Yankee blockade of our ports to get them for her. . . ." Mignonne's voice trailed away as her own ears rang with the false note.

She knew that she was chattering, but she must explain both to Robert and to Cooper.

"Even though Aunt Emma insisted, I wasn't going to wear them, but I knew that tonight I wouldn't be properly dressed without. . ." She waved her hand toward the bejeweled dancers.

"Even without gemstones, you'd be the loveliest jewel here," said Robert, surprising them so much with his eloquence that Cooper seemed struck dumb.

The orchestra leader had raised his baton, and in that moment before it came down, Robert bowed over her hand, asked permission to dance, and whirled her away, leaving Cooper standing in empty-handed amazement.

Swaying to the lilting rhythm of the "Blue Danube Waltz," Robert swung Mignonne in wide circles right, circles left, away from Cooper. They disappeared into intermingling colors and sounds.

In each other's arms at last, they clung, forgetting everyone but themselves. She relaxed in his embrace, trusting him to guide her through the elegant patterns.

Was this dizziness from the whirling and the mirrored lights? Or was it from Robert's nearness? His lips were against the curls on her forehead. What was he murmuring? She could not hear above the swelling of the music, the beating of her heart. She closed her eyes. Oh, let it be some pledge that would last beyond this night.

Lifting her lashes, fanning back the corners, she gazed into Robert's face bending close over hers. Open-mouthed, breathless, she said nothing, but his blue eyes penetrated the dark depths of hers. His tenderness quickened her hope that he understood her longing.

For timeless moments they did not realize that the music had ended. Before he could release her and either of them could think clearly, Cooper had found them. He demanded her next dance.

As Cooper rushed her away from Robert, she looked back wistfully. She wanted more time in Robert's arms. Even in worldly Saratoga, balls ended at midnight. Fear stabbed her. Only a few more tomorrows and this dream world would be gone.

She did not want to be with Cooper. The way he held her was insistent, forcing her to pull back. When he leaned too close, she smelled a whiff of alcohol.

Cooper's flirtatious remarks embarrassed her. Wondering if some of his innocent-sounding words held a double meaning, she was afraid to laugh or respond. His arrogant handsomeness reminded her of Paul.

Paul. How long it had been since she had thought of him! Now, as her feet stumbled through the intricate figures of the German, she made herself remember.

Paul had awakened her to first love, but she had been in love with romance much more than with Paul. She had ached for him to care, but she hadn't really liked him.

She liked Robert. He was a friend. Why hadn't someone told her how important friendship was to enduring love?

Drawing back from Cooper, Mignonne searched for Robert. There, in a corner beyond the giddy dancers, he stood quietly waiting. Her dark eyes, large, luminescent, an open window to her heart, conveyed her love across the room.

Robert's smooth face lighted with an answering smile, and he started toward her to claim her once again.

Happily they eluded Cooper. Others wanted her waltzes, but each time she danced with someone else, Mignonne was all the more eager for Robert. The ball was passing far too quickly.

When clapping signaled intermission, they were dismayed to see Cooper threading his way toward them. He carried two plates loaded with punch cups, cake, rye bread, and ham.

"I beat the crowd," he said. "Even the belle of

the ball must eat."

Robert frowned. "Is the other plate for me? I thought not." He hurried toward the table, but he was too late. A long line had formed ahead of him.

Cooper led Mignonne to an alcove.

Sitting down felt good. Her head was spinning. Her feet hurt. Too excited to eat, she nibbled at a piece of cake, feigning hunger to ignore Cooper's remarks.

He was sitting back in his chair, pulling up the corner of his mustache with an exaggerated motion. His lazy eyes were regarding her in a way that made her realize he had asked a question.

"Umm. What?" she murmured.

"I *said*, I want to be your escort for the masquerade that ends the season. I'm going as the devil in red suit and horns. With your black hair and white skin, you'd be spectacular in a red satin gown. Jezebel and the devil would take the prize for sure."

"I'd be a spectacle all right." She laughed hollowly. She avoided his probing eyes. Where was Robert? Silence stretched. Cooper was expecting an answer.

"Thank you for the invitation, but—but Robert. . ."

Robert had not actually asked her. He had merely told her about the masked ball.

"Robert and I. . .Yesterday at the races we discussed costumes. We haven't decided what to wear. . . ."

Frantically, she looked about for Robert. She

thought she glimpsed his curls above the crowd. Moments lengthened as she felt Cooper's expectancy. She had an uneasy sensation that seeing the rubies had increased his intentions to win her.

Robert emerged from the press of people. He had a plate in each hand, and a dazzling creature was hanging on his arm.

Miss McPheeter's gown was a shade of pale yellow that exactly matched her hair. A diamond tiara perched atop the frizzed and crimped creation that was her hairdresser's work of art. Diamonds dangled from her ears and arms and neck. Her only flash of color was in the different stones set in rings upon every finger. She was looking at Robert as if she could eat him instead of the food he carried for her.

Oh, dear, thought Mignonne. *Did I take too much for granted? Am I going to be hurt again?* She cupped her hands around her cheeks. She could feel them flaming.

Sighing, she took a resolute breath and faced Cooper. She bestowed him with her most charming smile.

"Thank you for asking me, Cooper," she said sweetly. "But I had planned to go to the masquerade with Robert."

As she spoke his name, Robert was standing beside her.

He cleared his throat. "Miss Wingate, I believe you know Miss McPheeter."

"How do you do?"

"How do you do?"

The girls nodded coolly to each other.

"I'd like to present my brother, Cooper Edgefield. He just arrived, and he doesn't know a soul here. You two share an interest in racing."

Settling down in a cloud of fluttering golden chiffon, the beauty cooed, "Ohhh, so many Mr. Edgefields, and I just simply can't decide which one is handsomest. I believe I'll sit down and eat to think about it. I'm simply famished."

Robert remained standing like a pillar. "Miss Wingate, if you won't think me rude," he said in a formal tone, "your cheeks are quite pink. Are you a bit overheated? May I take you out for some air?"

Mignonne stood so quickly that she nearly upset her plate. She did not need food.

When they were beyond earshot, she burst out laughing, "I don't have to sit down and eat to think about it. I know who's the *cleverest* Edgefield."

Robert grinned. "They deserve each other."

They stepped outside. The rain had stopped. The covering of striped awnings had been removed from the bridge. Now the open arch was outlined by the orange and scarlet and rose of softly glowing Chinese lanterns.

They strolled up the carpeted way and stopped at the crest. Leaning over the rail amid the fragrant treetops, they looked at the night sky. The clouds had blown away. The stars seemed near enough to touch. He stood behind her, and her head found rest on his shoulder. His arms felt strong, comforting as they closed around her.

"You rescued me just in time," she said dreamily. "I was struggling not to tell a lie."

"A lie?" he murmured, nibbling at the tendrils of hair that were slipping down the back of her neck.

"Um." She could hardly breathe, but she must clear this from between them. "Cooper asked me to the masquerade."

Robert stiffened. She tried to turn toward him, but his arms locked her against him.

"I told him you—Well, you didn't actually ask . . . I didn't want to tell an untruth. So I just said I'd planned to go with you."

The fierceness of his arms relaxed. Exhaling, he released her.

"If I assumed too much—" Tears rushed to her eyes. "If you had other plans—or Miss McPheeter asked you. . ."

She faced him. His eyes were shining, too. He unfolded the fists that she had clenched in sudden misery and kissed her palms.

"I hope this means more than that you're too smart to go with Cooper," he said huskily.

Seeing the muscle in his jaw working nervously, she sensed that she had been right. Cooper had been toying with her, and his flirtation was part of an ongoing game to take away what belonged to his younger brother.

She stroked Robert's tense jaw with soothing fingers and whispered, "It means that and a great deal more." Her radiant face, her soulful eyes expressed the love that would always put Robert first.

"Then you do feel as I do! I want to spend every hour of every day with you for—"

"Yes, oh, yes, Robert!"

His arms enclosed her at the same moment she reached up. Standing on tiptoe, she was at last able to twine her fingers in his hair. She clasped his curls with loving hands and tugged at them as he kissed her.

He held her back, gazing into her lovely face. "Mignonne Wingate, I love you."

"Robert Edgefield, I love you."

She lifted her lips, her heart to him. He kissed her tenderly at first and then with rising emotion.

She knew that she would never forget that moment. For the rest of her life she would remember that on the ninth day of August they had declared their love and Robert Edgefield had kissed her on a bridge that lifted them among the stars.

fourteen

The clouds returned in the night, and dawn on the tenth of August was unseen. Thin mists settled close around the upper stories of Congress Hall, which seemed, itself, to be sleeping. Even though the ball had ended at midnight, high excitement had been packed into those few short hours. Many Cinderellas and their Prince Charmings had lingered long on the bridge gazing at the stars. Now, morning was breaking, but no one wanted to shatter the spell by getting up. The few servants stirring about were tiptoeing.

Mignonne roused, dozed, tried to open her eyes. She wanted to remember Robert's kisses. She smiled, stretched deliciously, and snuggled back under the covers. She pulled the pillows around her, imagining they were Robert's arms. She felt warm, safe, wrapped in the security of his love.

She wanted to get up. To see him. She would waste no more time in doubting. Hadn't he said he wanted to see her every hour of every day? They would make the most of each day left here, and then—and then?

But for now it was still dark. She had danced a hole in her slippers, and her feet burned. She yawned. She would take one more little nap.

140

Laughing voices rising from beneath her window awakened her at last. Carriages were creaking by on their way to the spring. Sunshine was calling people outdoors to stroll amid the fragrant fir trees and freshly washed flowers.

Dressing quickly because it was time for the midday meal, Mignonne hurried to the dining room, eager to see Robert. She had never felt so happy.

None of the Edgefields appeared.

She lingered, eating another dessert. Still they did not come. She wandered down to the spring, hoping at every turn to see Robert.

With nothing to do, she went back to her room. Having finished her book, Mignonne felt fidgety. She rode down in the elevator three times, peering down, expecting to see Robert's face looking up.

Circling the lobby, she glimpsed Cooper going out the side door. She hurried to catch up. She could ask him if something was wrong.

At mid-step, she stopped. Hopefully, Cooper's attention was now on Miss McPheeter and her diamonds. Mignonne knew that she was too unsophisticated for Cooper's taste, but on the other hand, if he were merely trying to bedevil Robert, he might not give up on pursuing her. She would risk nothing that he might do to tease Robert or make him jealous.

Dodging behind a potted palm, she slipped out on the piazza.

Endine, who had gotten up before her, had been to the hairdresser. Her ridiculous hair had now achieved tangerine, and she allowed a few curls to escape the turban. She had toned down her freckles with rice powder and was putting on a worldly air, flirting with an old oil baron. She was desperately trying to make a new conquest now that Pietro was gone because she did not intend to miss the masquerade that ended the season.

Chuckling and shaking her head, Mignonne thought that Endine's heart had mended rather quickly. She turned back into the lobby, where she found a magazine. She took it to the bench in the parlor where she and Robert had read *Tom Sawyer.* She would simply wait.

Turning pages idly, she dreamed over the details of last night. Always—always, she wanted to remember how it had felt to go to a ball.

Eyes half closed, she sighed; then, as if she were awakening for the first time, her eyes flew open. Her heart had sensed his presence.

Robert was smiling tenderly. He sat with his arm on the bench beside her, holding her close. His lips brushed her hair.

"Mmmm," Mignonne said blissfully. Robert laughed. He kissed the tip of her nose.

"I only have a moment," he said softly, as if he hated to break the comfortable silence.

"While we were at the dance, Pa had a visitor. He mentioned seeing Cooper."

"Oh, my!"

"Yes."

"Oh, Robert, I told y'all it was wrong to lie,"

"I know. I wasn't lying—exactly. I just put off telling him until after the ball. I didn't want anything to prevent me from taking you."

"So now it's my fault," she said, bristling.

"No, no—but Pa had an angry scene with Cooper when we got in from the dance. He fell alarmingly ill."

"Because Cooper lost so much money?"

"Pa doesn't know that part yet. Because he risked Combahee. He's from fine Arabian stock. As I told you, we're trying to raise horses. We're depending on Combahee for bloodline."

She looked up at him questioningly. "But doesn't it make a name for the farm just to have a horse in the race?"

"You've been listening to Cooper."

"Well, it made sense. Are you sure you and your father aren't too closed to his ideas?"

Robert frowned at her.

"Don't you remember the steeplechase? With all the jumps, it's extremely dangerous. Don't forget about the horse that broke his leg. They had to shoot him."

"Oh!"

"It's one thing when you can afford to risk a horse. Quite another when you have only one. Anyway. I must get back. Pa was violently sick for the rest of the night. I shouldn't have left him now, but—oh, darling I couldn't bear it without seeing you. I had to have one kiss."

"I was saving it for you."

"Pretty sure of yourself, weren't you?" he teased.

His soft mustache brushed her cheek. She sat primly because there were so many people in the parlor.

"I wish we could find a place with a little privacy so I could kiss you properly."

Mignonne's eyes sparkled. "I know a spot. Cooper showed me."

"Oh." Robert drew away. "And what else did my brother show you?"

Mignonne looked at him seriously. "Robert Edgefield, you are not sure enough of yourself. What Cooper showed me is how very much I love you."

With springing steps, they hurried to the park and found the path that was secluded by tall shrubs.

His arms enwrapped her. Not caring if someone walked by, she returned his kiss with commitment of her love.

Emboldened, Robert kissed her again, pouring out his grief, his longing, his need. Stirred as she had never been before, Mignonne leaned back to catch her breath. She pressed her fingers over his face as if she wanted to memorize each line. Reaching up to twine his curls, she responded to his lips. No longer the kind of kiss to end when the clock struck midnight, these kisses told her she wanted to wake up each day with him and help him face gray dawns. Ceasing to dream of ball gowns, she had fleeting thoughts of aprons, and baking, and oh, yes, lots and lots of children.

At last he sighed and reluctantly started away. Turning, he saw her beguiling face and hurried back to kiss her again.

"You do understand?" he said, burying his face against her neck. "I meant what I said about wanting to spend every minute with you, but I'm worried to death about Pa. This afternoon, duty calls."

She knew how much he loved the sweet old man. She had felt the moisture in his eyes. But her disappointment was sharp. Not trusting her voice, she nodded and smiled, blinking furiously to hold back tears.

Then he was gone.

While the women had been busy at their matchmaking and the young men had played at love, Colonel Wadley and his old cronies had sat in the sun on the piazza, talking and dealing in railroads. The cool, dry air had aided his breathing. Drinking daily doses of the Congress water had helped. He was in fine spirits. He had made a recent acquisition of another railroad. By owning additional lines, he could protect the Central. He could funnel most of Georgia's cotton and timber into the port of Savannah.

His old friends did not mind him telling them again how he had begun as president of the Central Rail Road when it consisted of track twisted around pine trees and burned bridges left by Sherman's bummers. The Yankees had destroyed three hundred miles of railroad and everything else in their path across Georgia. This destruction had brought the Confederacy to its knees.

But now, Wadley's prosperous railroad had expanded to over two thousand miles.

His friends praised him that he had accomplished this with honesty and fairness, never succumbing to the swindles, grabbing, and even bloodshed with which many other rail lines were involved. They lamented that this prosperity had now focused the greedy attention of Wall Street upon him.

Time and again, Wadley had foiled General E.P. Alexander and his Wall Street syndicate from schemes to inflate the Central's stock.

Now Wadley's son and son-in-law arrived in Saratoga to tell him that the wily General had led his cohorts to initiate proceedings in the Ocean Steamship Company that they knew Wadley considered illegal.

Gleefully, Colonel Wadley rubbed his big hands together. "Now we have him! We can turn the matter over to the courts. Draw up papers for me to sign. This course of action will take a long time, but it will save the steamship line. With litigation pending, a restraining order will stop the general!"

Colonel Wadley's once powerful muscles sagged and his clothes hung on his massive frame. His hands shook as he signed the papers, but his mind was still sharp and quick. He was immensely pleased with himself for defeating his old nemesis. Now he could rest.

Around six o'clock on the evening of August 10,

he proposed that the family take a walk across town to visit friends from Savannah. With no beaus to squire them, Mignonne and Endine trailed along behind.

As they strolled along the tree-lined street, a passing carriage stopped. Three old acquaintances asked Colonel Wadley to join them for a drive.

"I'm going out with my wife," he replied.

"Leave your wife and go with us this time."

He laughed and told them jovially, "I never neglect my wife for anybody."

They walked along pleasantly for awhile, but then his steps began to lag as if it were an effort to lift his feet.

Rebecca frowned. She quietly suggested, "Perhaps, as it is late and the house rather far, we had better turn back and go another day."

They stopped. When he turned around, Mignonne saw his face with shock. It was as white as his silvery hair. He trembled, swayed. She thought of an ax felling a giant tree when the huge man fell upon the stones.

Rebecca shrieked. Endine screamed. Mignonne was frozen in silence. Sarah Lois knelt and cradled his head in her lap. He gasped once, then relaxed.

Rebecca ran into the street motioning to passersby. "Help! Please, help," she cried.

People came from all sides, crowding around.

"Give him air," his distraught wife pleaded.

With tear-filled eyes and gentle voice, her daughter looked up at her.

"He is dead."

Candles flickering at each end of the coffin could not dispel the feeling of darkness. The sickening sweetness of lilies was heavy in the stifling, airless room. Mignonne had never visited an undertaker's establishment. She had never looked down into a coffin.

In his dark, plum-colored suit and broad-collared linen, Colonel Wadley looked as he always had. The lines of his face had only eased into calm, into brightness.

Her throat worked convulsively. Surely they were mistaken. Surely he was just asleep.

The quiet was unbearable. She wanted to cry out, to fling herself upon Sarah Lois. But the tall woman was moving about taking care of everything, shepherding the dazed Rebecca, who moved in a state near collapse.

A brisk, sharp-eyed man strode into the room. Who? Those bushy black whiskers. Oh, yes. William Vanderbilt.

Mignonne clenched her fists as numbness broke open into overwhelming anger. Why did evil men prosper and someone so good as Colonel Wadley have to die?

She stumbled away from the coffin. She must have air.

She sat on the street curbing with her head in her hands. Death made everything so different. She remembered no grief at Grandma's passing. Only brief fright at strange happenings and childish acceptance. But now. . .it seemed as if Colonel Wadley was everyone's father.

Father? What of Robert's father? Was Robert experiencing something like this? She had not been understanding enough of his concern. *Oh, I hope I didn't show my disappointment at not being with him today!*

Yesterday. It was after midnight, the eleventh. *Yesterday.*

Through the black night, they moved automatically, obeying Sarah Lois's quiet commands to pack up their things.

When her trunks were ready to be transported to Mr. Vanderbilt's private car, which he had kindly offered, Mignonne dressed in her traveling costume. Head aching, she crept onto her bed.

Brief sleep only made her groggy. In the thin dawn, she paced her room, ringing her hands. She could not leave without telling Robert goodbye. It was not proper for a lady to go to a man's room. But she must!

She went down into the darkened lobby and inquired the number of the Edgefield's suite. When she found the door, it bore a sign, "Please, do not disturb."

She must. She could not leave without seeing Robert! Hurting, she raised her hand to tap.

What if Francis Edgefield were dying?

Mignonne leaned her forehead against the door. Robert had said he wanted to be with her every hour of every day. But they had missed yesterday. If only they had known it would be their last day!

Oh, dear God, she prayed, *I had thought Robert was the one You had prepared to be my husband.*

Feet dragging, she walked down the corridor. At the elevator, she stopped, remembering each word, each kiss as they stood on that beautiful bridge. In her eagerness to declare her love, she had interrupted him. He had not said forever. Maybe he only meant every hour of every day of the Saratoga season. And now, too soon, their dream world had ended.

Back in the lobby, she went to a writing desk and penned a quick note explaining their sudden departure.

Willing the elevator to hurry, she retraced her steps. Somewhere she heard a clock striking. The train would be leaving. Picking up her skirts, she ran pell-mell along the hall.

She slipped the letter under Robert's door, knocking softly, waiting. Maybe he would see it and open the door.

"Oh, Robert," she whispered, "J'aime et j'espere." She placed her palms, her wet cheek against the door.

Hopes dying, she turned away. She must join the family at the depot.

Even at such an early hour, Mr. Vanderbilt was there. Perhaps there was more goodness in him than she had thought. They were grateful for the seclusion of his private car. It was good to escape the crowd, but there was no relief from the clanging bells and blasting whistles. They echoed inside Mignonne's aching head until it seemed it must surely burst.

The Grand Union Depot in New York City seemed all noise and confusion. The stunned family was met and helped to change trains. Their precious burden was transferred to a special coach provided by friends from Colonel Wadley's Central Rail Road. In it, they were to travel to Atlanta.

The silence of the Atlanta depot made it even worse than the noise of New York. It was the saddest place Mignonne had ever seen. The walls of the cavernous station and all of the Central engines had been draped in black bunting.

The engine W. M. Wadley stood waiting with a special train sent from Savannah. It had all of its bright brass fittings covered with the black bunting of mourning. The engine was manned by old friends and pulled a coach for the family and one filled with railroad officials.

Suddenly every bell of every engine standing in the depot clanged. Bells continued to toll as the coffin with its silver plate and handles was transferred. It was carried between lines of employees to a baggage car walled up with black and white cambric.

As she followed the family to their coach, Mignonne's shock turned to uncontrollable weeping. She prayed that she could keep the tears silent and not sob out loud.

The W. M. Wadley rolled quietly through Georgia's red clay hills. No whistle blew. None was needed. At crossroads and stations, people stood waiting with quiet reverence. Silently they bared bowed heads, honoring the man as the train passed.

They reached Bolingbroke at last. The W. M. Wadley's brass bell was uncovered. It tolled to let the waiting household at Great Hill Place know they had arrived.

The large oaken box was taken into the parlor. William Morrill Wadley lay in state. People filed silently by. Plantation laborers, black and white, the poorest employees, the servants, joined the procession with officials from every department of the railroad who had come on another train from Savannah.

With the important people from Savannah was Colonel Estill, president of Wadley's favorite charity, the Union Society of Bethesda Orphanage. It was there that the Wadley's had found Libba Ramsey, who was also a guest on the special train.

No longer looking like a pinched-faced orphan, Libba walked beside her husband, Daniel Marshall. Smut-black curls still tumbled over her forehead, but her cheeks were full and pink. Her blue eyes were radiant in her love for Daniel in spite of her grief for the dear man who had helped her find her family.

Another train arrived bringing people from Macon. Every business there was closed by mayoral proclamation. Every bell in Macon was to toll from three 'til half-past three.

At three o'clock, the carryall was at the door. Slowly it was drawn by Colonel Wadley's prized roan horses to the family cemetery. Mourners walked behind it into the peaceful woodland.

Mignonne was shaking with emotion. She saw that Libba was no longer afraid to cry. Her tears were streaming down her cheeks. As Mignonne joined them, gentle, funny Daniel put an arm around each of them. But seeing their love only made her weep the more for herself.

She had lost all touch with Robert. Where was he? Did he find her note? What more would they have said if they had known they were seeing each other for the last time?

It was August 14. The scene in the woodland could not be real. It should suddenly turn into the gay masquerade.

But this was real. Colonel Wadley's sons were laying him in his grave. His brother Dole was throwing in a sprig of red clover because he loved it so much.

His pastor of Christ Church in Macon completed the service. A man and woman began to sing, "Write, write, write, Blessed are the dead who die in the Lord, for they shall rest from their labors."

fifteen

Mignonne's footsteps echoed hollowly on the stone steps that descended the terraces of the Great Hill Place garden. The throng that had attended the funeral was gone. Emptiness overwhelmed her.

She was not really sure why she had lingered one more day. Endine had already left to visit Paul.

And aggravate Victoria, Mignonne thought sourly.

She felt out of sorts, miserable. Sinking to a bench in the paved center area, she ached with tiredness, yet she seemed about to burst with frustration.

With dulled eyes she looked at the sculpture of the winged messenger Hermes. What of her message to Robert? Did he receive it?

Oh, if only he had seen my note and opened the door! If only I could have hugged him goodbye.

Jumping up, she could not stay in this place where Libba and Daniel's wedding had been. She could almost smell the orange blossoms, almost hear the joyous music.

Weddings! As sad a thought as funerals. She had dreamed of her wedding, but she had never thought of funerals. Now death and the reality of eternity stared her in the face.

Running downward, Mignonne left the formal garden and followed the woodland path.

At the creek, Paul's presence seemed to press upon her. Her cheeks flamed with the memory of her foolish flirtation. She covered her face with her hands, remembering, knowing now that she had not really been in love with Paul. She had been young, excited by him, infatuated with love itself.

She breathed a prayer of thankfulness that her mother's biblical admonitions had made her keep her emotions and her behavior in check.

Now her heart had grown. Robert had shown her the width and depth that love could take. She would love him forever—even if she never saw him again.

Turning, she climbed up the steep garden a different way. She stepped onto a new level she had not explored.

A row of hollies concealed the contents of this terrace. She entered through a narrow gate and discovered a secret garden.

Sarah Lois was sitting on the coping around a pool of goldfish. Her hand trailed idly in the water. Her plain face was crumpled with grief. She looked up slowly, dazed.

"I'm sorry." Mignonne backed away. "I didn't mean to intrude."

"No. Wait! Join me. I thought I wanted to be alone, but suddenly I'm too lonely."

Mignonne sat on the opposite edge of the small pool. The flashing red-gold fish flipped its tail and hid beneath a lily pad.

"I know you're exhausted," Mignonne said softly. "You've looked after everything and everybody. But then, we all take you for granted. We never realize that you spend your life in Christian service."

"A serving Christian is a happy Christian," Sarah Lois replied quietly.

They sat so still that the fish came out and began to feed.

Mignonne clenched and unclenched her fists. "You seem to know just how to deal with your emotions. I feel so—so angry!"

Sarah Lois's smile was wan. "Just now I wasn't dealing as well as you think. It's an overwhelming feeling that I don't have a Papa anymore. I spent my energies helping with his business. Now I don't have a job to do. . . ." She lifted empty hands and let them fall into her lap.

After long moments, she seemed to remember Mignonne.

"As to your anger, it's a natural part of grief. First comes shock, a numbness that helps you endure. Then anger. That's why people should never make decisions and changes too quickly after a death."

"But why does such a good man have to die while corrupt men, whose evil harms so many people, have all the power?"

"All the power? Oh, no. Very little, really, and only for a time. God has the power of eternity."

"But what is God's responsibility for all the hungry people?"

"They are not God's responsibility. They are ours. The task He sets before us. Christians are Christ's hands on earth."

The solitude of the warm summer night settled around them as Mignonne tried to absorb Sarah

Lois's wisdom.

"As to Father's passing, Dr. Clark warned that his heart was diseased beyond the reach of medicine. We knew he might live on or go at any time or place. I guess I simply forgot that he was mortal."

Tears trickled down Sarah Lois's cheeks, but she smiled at Mignonne.

"Perhaps you have set me a new task. Your questioning makes me know that his zeal in fighting corruption and keeping his railroad out of the hands of speculators should be remembered. In only a few short years, he turned the Central Rail Road from a pile of burnt crossties and track twisted around pine trees into nearly two thousand miles connecting the heart of Georgia with Savannah and New York."

Sarah Lois sat erect. Her dark eyes began again to snap with inner fire.

"Father built his railroad across the South with honesty and good for all concerned. This was at the same time that Indians and outlaws plagued trains in the West and swindlers and speculators stole far greater sums from Eastern railroads."

"People should know that in an era of scandals and corruption there was one man who stood for what is right," said Mignonne. "It is good to remember we are not alone in our faith."

"I shall write a book!" Sarah Lois dried her tears, invigorated.

"But even more lasting than that—his loving employees are erecting a statue in Macon at Mulberry and Third. For years to come it will overlook the river and the railroads. With his likeness struck in bronze, people shall not forget his integrity."

Grasping Mignonne's hand, she led her up the granite steps.

"Never fear, Mignonne. Evil may seem to rule for a day and deny the reality of God. But there is one valid argument against the doubters, a Christian character.

"And, oh, my dear, the influence of such a character does not die."

Would she ever see it again? Bolingbroke had been important because of Colonel Wadley. There had been trains coming and going constantly. What would happen now?

The mail train was arriving. Mignonne wished that she could wait for one more mail. There had not even been a letter of condolence to the Wadley family from the Edgefields. Seeing the sacks of mail unloaded, she had a wild desire to run back, to pour the contents on the ground, to search for some word from Robert. But her coach waited, momentarily sidetracked. The conductor was waving his arm, beckoning her to hurry.

"All aboard," he commanded.

As the train chugged slowly across Georgia westward toward Alabama, Mignonne felt drained of youthful excitement. At last they were on the trestle spanning the Chattahoochee, home.

She could hardly wait to climb into her canopied bed and close the curtains.

Waking up at last, Mignonne stretched. The ache in her bones from the rough train ride had diminished. The emptiness in her heart remained.

Mignonne pushed aside the filmy draperies of her bed. Already the morning was hot. She sighed. Being at home had not brought the peace she sought. She gathered up the organdy curtains and tied the pink ribbons. Then she leaned her head against the bedpost.

This had been her mother's girlhood bed. It had been wet with her tears, too. Mignonne knew that both Grandma and the river had come between Lily and Harrison. The belvedere of Barbour Hall, the Edwards' family home, had been Lily's sanctuary. There she had read her Bible and watched the drought-lowered river, praying for her lover's safe return.

With little hope, but lacking any other direction, Mignonne decided to go there. At least she would find solitude. Maybe a breeze. She dressed, took her Bible from her nightstand drawer, and trudged across town. Listless in the steamy heat, she began the climb up the hill to Barbour Hall.

Kitty opened the double doors to the cool marble foyer. Mignonne hugged her old nursemaid and murmured a greeting. Kitty had been a part of her life for as long as she could remember. She realized the emotional girl was in no mood to talk.

As much as she liked Adrianna, Mignonne was glad that the young matron and little Foy were not at home. She proceeded upstairs. Grandpa had built the house so that a draft of air flowed upward to the rooftop and out through the open windows of the belvedere. Even so, the glassed room was hot.

Wiping beads of perspiration on her upper lip, Mignonne remembered the cool afternoon at the lake. She and Robert had come to know each other. They had shared their hearts and minds and souls like two old friends.

She recalled Sarah Lois that day. She had seemed so young and carefree as they ate everything at the restaurant and rowed on the moonlit lake. Was she satisfied with her life as a spinster? The children of her brothers and sisters had given her their loving remembrance at the funeral. But was she really happy with no children or home of her own?

Once, in a sentimental moment, Sarah Lois had told how she had fallen in love with a man on a cross-country train. Duty had separated them, but she had always remembered that she was loved.

As I have been loved, Mignonne thought. Loving Robert had awakened her to the possibilities of life. She relived the night on the bridge of dreams. She whispered their words of love. She could nearly feel his curls in her hands, almost taste his lips. Her heart had opened in loving another, and she would never be the same.

I have this to remember: that once, once I was loved by Robert Edgefield and kissed among the stars.

Face wet, Mignonne sat down at the small table and opened her Bible with determination. It was marked where she had left it for a Sunday school lesson on the fifteenth chapter of Romans.

"We then that are strong ought to bear the infirmities of the weak, and not to please ourselves."

Colonel Wadley quoted that. But he and Sarah Lois were so strong, while I—while I please myself!

"For even Christ pleased not himself. . . ," she continued reading.

Self. Had she always thought of self first? Not of Robert or his father's needs. Not of God. *Have I not found peace because self has separated me from God's voice?*

She had enjoyed a lovely childhood nurtured in home and at church. She had accepted Jesus as Savior and friend at a young age. Dear old Uncle Jonathan had baptized her. But had she failed to grow in Christ? It was easy to live on the goodness and service and prayers of her parents.

It was as if she had accepted a beautifully wrapped gift, unwrapped it, and left it unused.

"A happy Christian is a serving Christian," Sarah Lois had said.

But what ability and strength do I have to serve?

Mignonne's eyes dropped to the page again. "Now the God of hope fill you with all joy and peace in believing, that ye may abound in hope through the power of the Holy Spirit."

God would provide the task. The presence of His Spirit would provide the power.

"Dear Lord, forgive me for not growing," Mignonne prayed fervently. "Help me to grow in service for Thee."

She could feel a warm sense that God had heard

and would answer her prayer. Joy burst upon her.

She stepped out of the glassed room onto the surrounding walkway. From this lofty tower, it seemed she could touch the sky. She leaned far out over the balustrade. With shining eyes, she traced the path of the Chattahoochee as it raced to its rendezvous with the sea.

She had rushed through her life. Now she would wait for God's command. She felt at peace. God's hands controlled her destiny.

Mignonne looked down. A handsome young man was striding by the red cedars at the gate.

It was her brother, Beau. He shouted to her, but the hot wind snatched away his words.

She cupped her hand to her ear to show she had not heard.

He held up a letter, black-bordered, a death message. He waved his arm, motioning her to come.

sixteen

When Mignonne and Beau arrived at home, they found their parents waiting for them in the parlor.

"My sister Jeanne's husband has drowned," Harrison Wingate told them. "He was an experienced navigator, but drought has lowered the Tombigbee River, and his steamboat went aground. It ripped a big hole. Water was rushing in, and he went below to try to stanch the flow." He shook his head sadly. "He went down with his boat."

"Oh, poor Aunt Jeanne!" exclaimed Mignonne, appalled.

"Having no children, she must feel so alone," said Lily.

"Her telegram sounded as if she is in great distress," Harrison replied. "We must leave for Demopolis at once."

"You don't have to go, dear," said Lily, going to Mignonne, who had grown pale, and smoothing her black hair. "You're too exhausted to make the trip clear across Alabama and too upset to attend another funeral. Why don't you stay with Emma? Jeanne will understand."

"She'll be too distraught to notice," agreed her father. "Jeanne is so impulsive. She will need someone to stay and help her—"

"I'll go. I'll stay to help. One should not make

163

decisions until after the first shock and anger of grief has passed."

Both parents stared at Mignonne in astonishment.

Heading west into the setting sun, the train took them to the beautiful old "Vine and Olive Colony" of Demopolis. From there, they traveled by carriage. The black dirt road took them along the Tombigbee River to Greenleaves Plantation. The federal style mansion, built by Harrison's parents in 1832, glowed with the patina of age. Mourners filled the beautiful red brick house, bringing food.

The sad process of a funeral was repeated. All too soon, everyone was gone, leaving Jeanne and Mignonne alone.

August passed into September. Mignonne did what she could to help. Moving with calmness, she had found the peace that comes from knowing God is in control. She realized now that disasters happen but God gives the strength to endure.

She thought so often of Robert. She felt secure in his love. She knew it would always be touching her even if they never saw each other again. She understood that honor kept him bound to his duty.

"Oh, Lord," she prayed daily, "If it be Thy will, may we serve Thee as man and wife? I place it in Thy hands."

Late one afternoon when she came across Aunt Jeanne's old croquet set, Mignonne's neck prickled. She could almost feel Robert's sweet, innocent kiss that had awakened love. Springing memories were so poignant that she had to be by herself.

She left the empty, echoing house and walked along the white limestone bluff.

Far below curled the trickling stream of the Tombigbee. Across the chasm to the west lay Indian lands. Mignonne had wept when she had read of the "trail of tears" that had taken Indians from Georgia to Oklahoma. The solemn red men and women she had seen selling their wares in Saratoga had touched her tender heart.

Fingering the trinket on the ribbon around her neck, she prayed, "Lord, are you calling me west to be a missionary to the Indians?"

She felt no warmth of reply. "Help me to know Thy will for me."

Robert understood his duty. What was hers?

Dreamily she began to sing the sad old ballad, "Lorena":

> *"For if we try we may forget,"*
>   *Were words of thine years ago.*
> *Yes, these were words of thine, Lorena—*
>   *They are within my memory yet—*
> *They touched some tender chords, Lorena,*
>   *Which thrill and tremble with regret.*
> *Twas not thy woman's heart which spoke—*
>   *Thy heart was always true to me.*
> *A duty stern and piercing broke*
>   *The tie which linked my soul with thee.*
> *A duty stern. . .*

A sob caught in Mignonne's throat. With tear-wet eyes, she looked down at the river. Still drought-low, it shut out steamboat traffic. If sudden rains came, they might not be enough to raise the river for steamers, and the black, canebrake mud could make roads impassable. Greenleaves would be isolated.

"Oh, Lord," she prayed, "Should I stop waiting to hear from Robert? If I don't write to him before winter comes, mail might not get through."

She did not know his address. She knew Combahee was named for a river in South Carolina. She knew one could sit on the porch and rock and look out across salt marsh. Suddenly she had an idea. She could send a letter by Sarah Lois. The proper spinster would, no doubt, think it unseemly for a lady to write a gentleman.

But I was the one who left abruptly, Mignonne reasoned. *The newspapers would have carried the story of Colonel Wadley's death, but Robert might not have found my note.*

She turned, discovering that she had wandered far down the bluff.

In the distance was someone following her footsteps.

Robert. The swinging of his hands confirmed the singing of her heart. She began to run.

Meeting her, he swooped her into his arms and suddenly she found home.

"Did you make me search the world to prove my love is forever? Every time I reached a place you had gone farther."

"Oh, Robert! I didn't mean to make you prove yourself. I knew the first moment I saw you that—"

Kisses interrupted words.

Sitting on the riverbank watching the sunset streak the blue with gold, they shared their searching.

"Haven't you received any of my letters?"

"No. I guess mail trains couldn't catch up." She dreaded to ask. "What news of your father?"

"Well," he said, taking a deep breath. "Cooper drove him into an apoplectic rage. He was in critical condition. I couldn't leave him as much as I wanted to look for you. Prayer and care saved him. He's better. Enough better that he sent me to find you. He said he needed your smile, but we didn't know what we'd be asking you to give up. . . ."

She wondered why his brows came down to shadow his deep-set eyes.

"I. . .my stop in Eufaula yielded your parents' blessing, too. Your mother even found we've a family connection through the Bethunes." He laughed uncertainly.

"I've been pressing west with only the thought of seeing your face. But. . .but now that I'm here . . .Your home is so warm and loving. Eufaula is so perfect. Now seeing you father's old family manor . . .Why, this plantation is so manicured that. . .I can't ask you to marry me—not without telling you . . ."

He was talking so slowly, so shyly that her eyes

grew wider trying to contain her excitement. With difficulty, she waited, squeezing her hands together.

"Pa's left side is paralyzed. My duty holds me on Combahee to care for him. I also have responsibility for my twin sisters. Ruth and Rubye are a handful. Perhaps they need a woman's touch. And the house—I told you it came through the war unscathed, but it's pretty run down since Mother died. We've been putting every penny back into the farm. Our country's seen hard times, but I'm full of hope for the future. We could make things grow and prosper if only I had you beside me."

He lifted a worried face, and his blue eyes searched hers earnestly. "I don't know if I can ask you to accept a less than perfect home. I wish I could offer you a Grand Tour of Europe, offer you—"

Mignonne laughed softly and her fingers reached up to smooth his cheek. She did not know what the girl she had been would have answered, but her woman's heart reached out with the tenderest of self-giving love.

"There is only one offer I would accept, a heart and mind and soul to share my love and joy and peace."

Her lashes fanned back from sparkling brown eyes, and her pixie face smiled impishly. "Listen! Isn't that mockingbird singing Mendelssohn? If you can't ask, I must.

"Robert Edgefield, will you marry me?"

acknowledgments

When I first read Sarah Lois Wadley's book, *A Brief Record of The Life of William M. Wadley* (November 12, 1813—August 10, 1882), I thought it an account by a doting daughter and too good to be true. Further research proved her correct. *The National Cyclopedia of American Biography* calls him "the unquestioned railroad genius of the South . . .who invariably placed the welfare of his company above his private interest." *The Macon Telegraph and Messenger* (August 11, 1882) stated: "Every bar of iron nailed upon the breast of Georgia is a monument to his foresight and industry; every engine a banner inscribed with his fame. The gentleman's name alone is a tower of strength."

After his death, the Central Rail Road was taken over by General E.P. Alexander and his Wall Street syndicate. It collapsed, having become part of the great financial scandal of the era of railroads and robber barons. *The Great Richmond Terminal* by Maury Klein gives details. Also of help was *America in 1876,* by Lally Weymouth, and *Certain Rich Men,* by Meade Minnigerode.

Wadley's railroad was salvaged and reorganized in 1895 as the Central of Georgia Railway by Hugh M. Comer, another man of integrity.

Thanks goes to Anne H. Rogers of Washington

Memorial Library in Macon for use of their extensive Wadley collection; to Harriet Bates, Lake Blackshear Regional Library; and to Jean Stamm, Saratoga Springs Public Library.

Information on Saratoga came from *The Daily Graphic*, Saratoga Springs, New York, July 21, 1875 and August 6, 1878; *Sparkles From Saratoga* by Sophie Sparkle, 1873; and *Saratoga Trunk* by Edna Ferber, 1941.

Colonel Wadley died in Saratoga and was carried in Vanderbilt's car as I have said. He and Sarah Lois were made to come alive for me by his great-granddaughter Anne Winship who took me to Great Hill Place at Bolingbroke.

Thanks go to Citizens Telephone Company, Leslie, Georgia; to Glenda Calhoun; and to John Cook, who helps in so many ways.

In Eufaula, Alabama, my Barbour Hall is based on Fendall Hall which is preserved as a museum by the state of Alabama.

On a recent spring afternoon, I was invited to the house to sign my series of river books. Of course, my central characters exist only for my readers and me, but for a little while, they, too, came alive through local people dressed in costumes. I wish all of you, my readers, could have attended this writer's fantasy come true.

JACQUELYN COOK

A Letter To Our Readers

Dear Reader:

In order that we might better contribute to your reading enjoyment, we would appreciate your taking a few minutes to respond to the following questions. When completed, please return to the following:

Rebecca Germany, Editor
Heartsong Presents
P.O. Box 719
Uhrichsville, Ohio 44683

1. Did you enjoy reading *Rivers Rushing to the Sea*?
   ☐ Very much. I would like to see more books
      by this author!
   ☐ Moderately
      I would have enjoyed it more if _____

   _____

2. Are you a member of *Heartsong Presents*? Yes   No
   If no, where did you purchase this book? _____

   _____

3. What influenced your decision to purchase
   this book? (Circle those that apply.)

Cover	Back cover copy
Title	Friends
Publicity	Other _____

4. On a scale from 1 (poor) to 10 (superior), please rate the following elements.

    ___Heroine   ___Plot

    ___Hero   ___Inspirational theme

    ___Setting   ___Secondary characters

5. What settings would you like to see covered in *Heartsong Presents* books?

_____

_____

6. What are some inspirational themes you would like to see treated in future books?_____

_____

_____

7. Would you be interested in reading other *Heartsong Presents* titles?   Yes   No

8. Please circle your age range:

Under 18	18-24	25-34
35-45	46-55	Over 55

9. How many hours per week do you read? _____

Name _____

Occupation _____

Address _____

City _____ State _____ Zip _____

·········· Presents ··········

__HP42 SEARCH FOR TOMORROW, *Mary Hawkins*
__HP43 VEILED JOY, *Colleen L. Reece*
__HP44 DAKOTA DREAM, *Lauraine Snelling*
__HP45 DESIGN FOR LOVE, *Janet Gortsema*
__HP46 THE GOVERNOR'S DAUGHTER, *Veda Boyd Jones*
__HP47 TENDER JOURNEYS, *Janelle Jamison*
__HP48 SHORES OF DELIVERANCE, *Kate Blackwell*
__HP49 YESTERDAY'S TOMORROWS, *Linda Herring*
__HP50 DANCE IN THE DISTANCE, *Kjersti Hoff Baez*
__HP51 THE UNFOLDING HEART, *JoAnn A. Grote*
__HP52 TAPESTRY OF TAMAR, *Colleen L. Reece*
__HP53 MIDNIGHT MUSIC, *Janelle Burnham*
__HP54 HOME TO HER HEART, *Lena Nelson Dooley*
__HP55 TREASURE OF THE HEART, *JoAnn A. Grote*
__HP56 A LIGHT IN THE WINDOW, *Janelle Jamison*
__HP57 LOVE'S SILKEN MELODY, *Norma Jean Lutz*
__HP58 FREE TO LOVE, *Doris English*
__HP59 EYES OF THE HEART, *Maryn Langer*
__HP60 MORE THAN CONQUERORS, *Kay Cornelius*
__HP61 PICTURE PERFECT, *Susan Kirby*
__HP62 A REAL AND PRECIOUS THING, *Brenda Bancroft*
__HP63 THE WILLING HEART, *Janelle Jamison*
__HP64 CROWS'-NESTS AND MIRRORS, *Colleen L. Reece*

Great Inspirational Romance at a Great Price!

Heartsong Presents books are inspirational romances in contemporary and historical settings, designed to give you an enjoyable, spirit-lifting reading experience. You can choose from 64 wonderfully written titles from some of today's best authors like Colleen L. Reece, Brenda Bancroft, Janelle Jamison, and many others.

When ordering quantities less than twelve, above titles are $2.95 each.